IT THAT HAS NO NAME

P. S. KESSELL

iUniverse

IT THAT HAS NO NAME

Author Credits: Pamela Kessell

iUniverse books may be ordered through booksellers or by contacting:

iUniverse
1663 Liberty Drive
Bloomington, IN 47403
www.iuniverse.com
1-800-Authors (1-800-288-4677)

ISBN: 978-1-5320-9186-5 (sc)
ISBN: 978-1-5320-9187-2 (e)

Library of Congress Control Number: 2020900326

Print information available on the last page.

iUniverse rev. date: 01/13/2020

This book is dedicated to my sister, Patricia; my son, Jim, my daughter, Breanna; and my friend Maya, who share my love for the horror genre, and to my mom and dad, who have helped in many ways to make this book possible.

CONTENTS

1

IT DANCES WITH THE HAMILTONS

October 1990

The old house suddenly became cold and still. Evie's breath was shallow and quick. She was still in shock over what had happened in the last few hours. She was hesitant to move, so she just stood there, breathing and staring into the space before her.

Then slowly, she moved forward, advancing toward her mother, who lay on the floor in front of her. She kneeled down on the floor beside her mother and whispered to her, hoping for a response. Yet there was no verbal response or movement to let Evie know that she was okay. Her mother just lay there. Evie cried and curled up next to her. She heard the sound of sirens coming from outside. They were getting closer and closer to her house.

A book, which was lying on the floor near them, caught her attention. Her mother had been reading from that book just before the lights had gone out that night.

Evie closed the book, picked it up, and carried it back to the hole in the brick wall from which her mother had taken it. It was a heavy book—almost too heavy for Evie to lift. The outside of the book had a gold emblem that was shaped like a musical note. Evie didn't know much about the book but did know that it was somehow very important. That's why she was returning it to where it had been hidden for what looked like a very long time.

Evie placed the book in the hole and covered it with bricks that were lying on the floor. While she did it, she heard faint whispers coming from the shadows in the room.

Then the police and emergency technicians arrived. Evie, who was in the basement, heard them upstairs. Some of them gasped for breath at what they saw. Others were checking for pulses where they thought they saw hope, only to find disappointment.

Evie began to cry again and returned to the floor to lie next to her mother. Her hope that her sister might be alive was shattered with each step she heard on the floor above her. They didn't seem to be in a hurry to rescue anyone.

Evie heard the creaking of the basement door as it was opened. She was hopeful that it was someone who could help her and her mother but fearful that it might just be a continuation of the hellish nightmare she had just experienced. She remained still and quiet. She saw lights and heard voices. The voices called out for someone to respond, but she remained quiet. The police officers began searching the basement and discovered that there were more bodies.

"We have two more down here," one police officer said.

Evie closed her eyes tightly, as she was afraid that this was not what it seemed. Tears welled up in her eyes. Was she being rescued or was this just another horrible hallucination?

She heard another police officer yell, "We have a live one here. She's just a little girl."

Evie felt him scoop her up in his arms and start to carry her away, but Evie yelled for her mother. The loud, screeching yell revealed just how terrifying her night had been. The officer tried to comfort her by telling her that she was okay and safe, but Evie did not feel safe.

The officer took her to an ambulance, where they checked her vitals and prepared her for transport to the hospital. Out of the corner of her eye, Evie saw the officers bring out a woman on a gurney. One of her arms dangled off the side of it. She realized that this was her aunt, and she fought the paramedics to try to get to her. Then, Evie felt a slight pinprick in her arm. Soon she was unable to cry out anymore. She slowly drifted off to sleep while still whispering her aunt's name.

Once Evie reached the hospital, Detective Warren Baker arrived and wanted to speak to Evie. Doctor Edward Jameson, Evie's emergency room physician, informed Baker that she had been sedated. She could not speak with him.

"You'll have to wait until she is ready to speak to you, detective," Jameson said.

"And when might that be?" Baker asked him.

Jameson replied, "She may be able to speak to you in the morning."

"Listen here. With all due respect, doctor, I have six dead bodies that came out of that house tonight, and that little girl is the only one who came out alive. I want you to understand how important it is that I speak to her as soon as possible, ya hear me?" Baker said. "Do you understand?"

Officer Jacob Barnes interjected, "C'mon Baker. You know the deal. We all do. There was nothing normal about that family or anything that went on in that house. Quite frankly, I'm surprised there were any survivors."

"But doesn't that make you want to know even more about what happened there tonight?" Baker replied.

"No! No, it doesn't! It makes me wanna go home, tuck my little girls in bed, and kiss my wife good night before she rolls over and goes to sleep," Barnes said.

Baker looked from Barnes to Jameson and back at Barnes again. The detective started to say something and changed his mind. He realized nothing that he said would convince either man to change his mind about what they believed had happened in the house that night.

"We need to notify Rebecca," Barnes said.

"That's easier said than done," the doctor responded. "She chose to marry and move away from here. She doesn't talk to anyone from here anymore."

"Well, we still have to find her," the detective said. "She needs to be here for Evie."

"What about Charlie?" the doctor said.

"Charles? Hell, no one has even seen him in five years," the officer said with a slight chuckle.

"Even after doing a thorough investigation, her father is still being listed as a missing person," the detective said. "He just disappeared without a trace. There's no finding him."

Suddenly, a horrifying scream came from Evie's room. The doctor, detective, officer, and nurses ran into her room. She was sitting up in bed with her eyes wide open, staring out into the space in front of her.

Unseen by everyone in the room except for Evie was Evie's mother, who was reaching out for her as her skin split from ear to ear. Her head was forced forward as something tried to come out of her body. From out of her neck emerged a male form covered in blood, which was dripping from him. He peeled back layers of her skin very slowly until he was no longer inside of her. Then he quickly transformed into a swarm of bees and flew into little Evie's mouth. She fell backward onto her bed and began to choke from something the medical team in the room could not see.

Baker helped to hold Evie down. For just a few moments, he made eye contact with her.

She looked up at him. It was as if she were looking through the eyes of a bee.

For just a few seconds, the detective swore that her head tilted upward toward his and her choking sound became more of a sinister chuckle. He jerked away, believing that his eyes and ears were playing tricks on him.

Evie's heart was beating faster and her breathing was much heavier. Her vitals had become critical. Evie was dying, and they could not seem to save her. They attempted to intubate her with no luck. Her trachea was blocked, but they didn't know by what. With every attempt, they failed.

Just like that, she was gone. The sound of her heartbeat flatlining on the monitor was deafening. Jameson pronounced Evie's death. "Evelyn Harrison. Date: October 13, 1990. Time of death: 11:10 p.m. Cause of death: respiratory arrest."

The men spoke very little afterward. They all seemed to realize that some things were best left alone and forgotten. That is what they decided to do with the night's events. Jameson told them that he needed to make his rounds. Baker told Barnes that he was headed to the morgue. Barnes took one last look upward at the hospital room where Evie had been asleep one hour earlier. Then he got into his police car and drove home to his family.

2 A NEW SCHOOL YEAR FOR KATIE

August 2018

On the last Monday in August, the Carrollton family began another first day of school. This year, Katie was starting her senior year, and it would be filled with excitement and many firsts: a car, homecoming, prom, and a real date. She could not wait for the year to begin. Well, sort of.

Her new car was actually her sharing her mother's car for an indefinite period. The title of homecoming queen usually went to a member of the school band, which Katie was not into or part of at all. Prom was something she would only attend if she had a date—preferably if it was with Robbie Montero. He was the cutest guy in the whole school and quarterback on the football team. He was also taken by one of the prettiest girls in the school, who was captain of the cheerleading squad.

Katie dreamed of her first real date. She desired it to be something a little more formal than homecoming. She wanted to go to a restaurant that she had to dress up for and that only included the two of them. That would be so much better than how she had been dating, which went something like the following.

"I will meet you over at your best friend's house, and we will hang out," the boy would say.

"Yeah, sounds great," she would say.

"Great! It's a date then," the boy would say.

"Great! I'll see you there," she would say.

That would be the definition of a date in high school these days. She was hoping for the real thing in her senior year—a new year with a real first date—which was something she had not yet experienced.

"Are you going to eat your breakfast or just stare at it?" Katie's mother asked.

Katie was so caught up in her daydreaming that she had forgotten she was supposed to eat and then leave for school. Now she was running late. She wouldn't be able to hang out with her friends before the day started. They always met under the same tree near the front of the main building.

"Mom, I'm late. Sorry, I gotta go," Katie said while heading out the door. Off to school Katie went, driving her mother's 2017 Nissan Altima.

Katie's mother, Christina, was of an average height and a slender woman, much like Katie was. She lacked physical strength but made up for it in mental ability. She was a smart woman with expensive taste but lived well within her means. The realty company that she owned was doing very well, and things kept improving for her.

She and her husband, Dr. David Carrollton, had lived in Suffolk County, Massachusetts, for several years before they had decided to move to her family's hometown near Salem. Katie's father was offered a position at Cornerstone Memorial Hospital—a position he could not refuse.

They had been in Salem for three years now and had been very happy with their decision to move there, despite the concerns of Christina's mother, Rebecca, who had feared that the family's history would repeat itself. Even she had finally come to admit that the move had been a good decision for the family.

Everyone had seemed to hit the ground running when the family moved to Salem. Katie had made great friends that she had kept since her first day of school. David Carrollton had been welcomed with open arms at the hospital, which had desperately needed a cardiovascular surgeon. Business at her mother's realty company had started out slowly but had soon picked up. The business had begun to sell older, larger properties in the area that had gone for high-dollar price tags. She and her husband had even flipped some of the homes to make a larger profit from the sales.

Only James, Katie's brother, had experienced some issues while trying to make friends when they moved to Salem. As the new kid, he was the victim of several pranks played on him by a class bully. Even that got better as James got older and a little bigger.

James had one true best friend, and that was what mattered most to him. His name was Tristan Templeton. Tristan was a cute ten-year-old with dark hair and dark eyes. He was full of swag for his age.

James and Tristan spent every waking moment on their technological gadgets. Even Katie and her friends turned to James and Tristan when they had technological questions and issues. Normally, Katie did not desire James's presence when her friends were around. However, he was widely sought after if for some reason she or her friends could not access the internet.

Fortunately for Katie, her mom did not insist that she take James with her on her first day of driving to school. She was running late and did not have time to take him and make it to class on time.

When Katie arrived at school, she pulled into the student parking lot. She located a parking spot in another row and just needed to get to it. By the time she did, someone else had already parked in it. She ended up parking in a space that was far from her first-period.

She went straight from her car to her first class.

What had started out as a great day suddenly took a turn for the worse. None of her friends were in her first-period. She saw Robbie and his girlfriend, Gloria Menendez, in there. Second and third periods were much the same. None of her friends shared a class with her. This had never happened to her before. She had always had classes with at least one of her friends. It was disappointing and gave her an uneasy feeling.

During fourth period, she again had no friends in class with her, but this time, someone caught her attention. A new boy who sat two rows over from her was introduced to the class as Chase Monroe from Boston. His hair was like glittering gold, and he had eyes as blue as Caribbean water. When he stood, he was tall and upright. He was very attractive and not just to Katie. Every girl in the room eyeballed him. He was a stark contrast to Robbie but equally as attractive.

When he was introduced, he was a little embarrassed, which caused him to reveal a very sexy grin. Katie knew she could not stake her claim on Chase. Melanie, her best friend, would surely do this, and Katie had already laid claim to Robbie. She decided that this was going to be an exciting school year or the worst school year ever.

The clouds in the sky had begun to roll in. They were dark gray, fluffy, and full. She hadn't thought that it was supposed to rain that day, but they looked like storm clouds. Soon she would go to the place in the cafeteria where she usually met up with her friends to have lunch, especially on rainy days when they had to stay inside. Now all she needed was the nerve to invite Chase to eat with them. She would invite him as soon as the class period ended.

After the bell had rung, Katie walked toward Chase, only to find that Gloria was headed toward him too. Both of them rushed to get there. Katie pushed a desk out of her way. They practically said his name at the same time, but Katie was persistent and won Chase's attention. She introduced herself and invited him to eat lunch with her and her friends, but he kindly declined.

"I was invited to eat lunch with the guys on the football team," Chase said. "I can't start out the year ditching them already. Can we get together another day?"

"Yes, absolutely! What position will you be playing on the team?" she asked.

"Wide receiver," he replied.

"Awesome! So lunch tomorrow?" she said.

"Yes, that works!" he replied. "But let's not wait until then to talk again. Here's my number. If you aren't too shy, you can call or text me."

"Me, too shy? Ha!" Katie said.

"Good. Then we have a phone date at around eight o'clock?" Chase said.

"Yeah. Yes, we do," Katie said.

Chase had to hurry so that he could meet up with the football players. Katie needed to hurry so that she could meet her friends. She wanted to figure out why she was not in any classes with them. She heard Chase apologize to Gloria for not having time to talk to her. He told her that he would see her on the practice field after school. Katie was not jealous. Well, maybe she was just a little bit.

3 MELANIE STAKES HER CLAIM ON CHASE

The first day of school was not going to start as a typical day for Melanie Holcomb, Katie's best friend. She had just celebrated her seventeenth birthday, and her father, Johnathan, had surprised her with a new car. Today, she would be driving a black, 2018 Camaro convertible to school. Melanie believed that her father had purchased the gift as a way of apologizing for working on her birthday. She didn't care because she was used to it by now. He always worked and rarely knew where she was or what she was doing.

If he was not working, he was dating or chasing the next newly available woman in town. He was a handsome man who worked as an industrial engineer. He was available and wealthy, so he had plenty of women. By this point in Melanie's life, she was content with their relationship. He provided for her needs at home, and she got whatever she wanted without hassles or arguments.

Melanie arrived at school early enough to drive around and show off her new car. She beeped her horn several times and waved as she passed the cheerleaders and football players, some of whom she had dated. She parked her car up front so everyone would see her make her grand entrance. She walked over to her friends who had already arrived.

"Hey, Sandy, have you seen Katie this morning?" Melanie asked.

"No, I haven't seen her. It's getting late though," Sandy said. "Maybe we will find her in first period. Who do you have?"

They continued to make small talk until their friend Jay said that he had seen Katie in her mother's car. Sandy's boyfriend, Jeb, had yelled out to Katie, but Katie had not responded. Then the school bell rang, and all of the students moved toward their first-period classes.

It was lunchtime before Melanie saw Katie. Melanie walked into the cafeteria and toward the table she knew her friends would be at. They always chose the tables near the small windows by the exit door. Melanie walked up to the group and shared hellos with all of her friends. Within seconds, she heard Katie's excited voice as she was grabbed from behind.

"How did you like driving that new car to school

today?" Katie asked. "Did you have the top down? I bet you made quite an entrance."

"Yes, yes, and yes to all of it!" Melanie responded with an excited and impatient voice. "Have you seen him?"

"Seen who?" Katie asked.

Melanie couldn't believe that Katie was trying to act like there was no one special that she could have seen. Melanie knew it was impossible for Katie to have made it halfway through their day without seeing or at least hearing about Chase.

"Him. The new kid, Chase," Melanie said with bottled-up excitement.

"Oh, yeah. He is in my fourth-period class," Katie replied.

Because of the way Katie responded, Melanie thought that Katie was hiding the fact that she had a real interest in him. "And? Come on. He's fine, and you know it," Melanie said.

Katie couldn't really lie to her because her whole body was giving away how she really felt. However, she knew that the minute she admitted that he was cute, Melanie would stake her claim on him. Then Katie would be back to hoping for Robbie and Gloria to break up.

"Yeah, he's kind of cute," Katie said, trying not to seem that into him.

"Yes, he is, and he's all mine," Melanie said. "He's

in my second-period class. I exchanged notes with him all period. He gave me his phone number and told me to text him anytime. He has such dreamy blue eyes."

"Yeah, of course you can have him. I still have hope that Robbie and I will get together one day," Katie replied. "It could happen."

The bell rang for class to start. Katie did not know what she would do with the phone number in her pocket. She could not call or text Chase now. That would be a violation of the unspoken best-friend agreement.

She wondered, *what about the next day*? He was supposed to eat lunch with her. She would make it appear as though he had come to lunch with her from fourth period to meet up with Melanie. That would work as long as Melanie did not invite him to lunch with her. He might then reveal that he had already made lunch plans with Katie. That would ruin everything.

Katie could not think about that. She just had to focus on making it appear that her interest in him was for friendship alone. She would make up some excuse for not being able to call him. She would behave around him as she would around Jeb or Jay. It was no problem. She could handle it.

The end of the school day came and went. Katie wanted to meet up with her friends at the local ice-cream shop, but her mother needed the car, so she went home. When she got there, her mother asked her to come with her to run a few errands. Katie didn't really want to go, but her mother told her it would be worth her time, so she did. Her mother made James go too. Their first destination was about a thirty-minute ride down an old highway, so Katie settled in for a little nap while her mother drove.

4

THE HOUSE ON HIGHWAY 89

Katie felt the car come to a stop. After opening her eyes from her brief nap, she saw a tall rod-iron gate with lots of bushes that blocked much of her view of an older home. The house appeared to have been well kept. Her mother got out of the car and opened the gate. She got back into the car and drove up closer to the house. Katie, James, and their mother got out of the car and started looking around.

"This is a new listing for me," Katie's mother said. "I think that if your father and I invest a little money in her, we can make a good profit from this place."

"It's not too bad for an old house," Katie said.

"It really needs a good cleaning," Katie's mother added.

"Aw no, please tell me that's not why you dragged me along," James whined.

Christina and James placed the realty company's sign in the house's front yard and added a holder for some brochures and flyers for future open-house events. The house still needed to be remodeled before any events could be held.

"I will spend about two months remodeling some of the rooms. Then I will have it cleaned two weeks before the open house," she said. "I really have a good feeling about this house, Katie. Its history won't matter much once it has been renovated."

Katie asked, "What do ya mean by 'its history'?" However, Katie's mother had already walked away from her, and Katie was too tired to wonder much about it.

As her mother went upstairs to open a couple of windows to let fresh air in and her brother went wandering, Katie walked toward the kitchen. On the way there, she passed a door that made her pause. The hair on her arms stood up.

There was a chill in the air. She could see her breath in front of her. As she turned to look at the door, ice formed along the door's keyhole and handle. Then it seemed to spread across the door. It sent chills up and down her spine. It felt as if someone was tickling her spine with soft fingertips. She could feel the touch against her bare skin even though her shirt was covering that area. It was the creepiest thing she had ever felt.

She saw someone's shadow to the right of her but was too frightened to turn around and look. She was slowly turning her head to see what was behind her when her brother came around the corner and said that it was time to go. Whatever it had been, it had left in a flash.

"Did you see anything besides me in the hallway next to the door?" Katie asked.

"No," he replied, barely paying any attention to her.

She grasped his arm and questioned him more directly. "Did you see anything at all in the hallway with me? I mean anything," Katie said in desperation.

"No, I didn't. You're psycho," James responded. "Are you seeing ghosts? You're crazy."

"I didn't say anything about ghosts, jerk," Katie replied. She believed she must have imagined the whole thing.

As they were driving home, Christina, Katie's mother, told Katie not to get too excited as they made the next turn. Then Christina turned into the Nissan dealership's parking lot. Katie knew immediately what this meant for her and started screaming. Her mother's face lit up. Her brother yelled, "I want one too."

Katie turned to her mother and said, "Really? Are you serious? I thought I was going to have to wait awhile."

"Well, your father and I talked about it last night, and there are some conditions," her mother said. "First, you will have to take your brother to school every morning. He will be able to walk home with Tristan after school but must ride with you in the mornings. Second, you're not actually getting the new car. The new car is mine. You're getting this one. The new car is your father's birthday gift to me."

"Still, thank you, Mom. Thank you," Katie said. She was ecstatic. She had not been sure if she would see the keys to her own car until she left for college the following year.

"Do I have permission to go to Melanie's house for a quick visit to share my good news?" Katie asked.

"Yes, but don't be home too late," she replied. "You have school tomorrow." It was just like her mother to remind her of school as if she had forgotten.

Katie had almost made it out of the parking lot when her mother flagged her down and said those words every older sister hates to hear: "Take your brother with you."

"Oh, Mom, why?" Katie asked.

"Because I have to go by the hospital to see your father and run a few more errands before I go home. Please, Katie?" her mother asked.

"Get in, James, but I don't want to hear one word from you," Katie said, "and no hitting on Melanie."

"Okay, I get it. I don't want to go with you either," James said.

As Katie drove to Melanie's house, she was still thinking about the eerie feeling she had felt in that

26

house. She parked in front of Melanie's house. She saw Melanie in the upstairs window and waved to her to come outside. Katie was dangling her keys from her hand with a great big smile on her face. Soon, both girls were jumping and screaming with excitement. Earlier, Katie had told Melanie that it would be awhile before her parents would give her a car.

"This is so exciting," Melanie said. "Now when we go somewhere, we'll have to choose whose car to take."

Katie laughed. "No, we'll take yours every time." Both girls laughed. Then the conversation turned to boys and parties.

"By the way, Sandy called earlier," Melanie said. "Her parents are not going anywhere next month for their anniversary. They canceled their plans to Mexico."

"Oh no. That's where we planned to have the first party of our senior year," Katie said. "What'll we do now?"

"I know what you can do," James said.

"Shut up and mind your own business," Katie said.

The girls moved away from the car to keep James from hearing their conversation. James stuck his head out of the window while the girls continued to talk. "I'm serious," he said even louder. "I have a great idea."

"Leave us alone," Katie yelled.

Because she was desperate, Melanie became interested in what he had to say. "Wait just a minute, Katie. Let's see what Peanut has to say." Peanut was

Melanie's nickname for James. "This better be worth it, Peanut."

"Today, Mom showed us a house that she plans to have remodeled and cleaned within six weeks. You can hold your party there," James said.

"No, we cannot hold a party in one of the houses Mom is trying to sell," Katie said.

"Wait! Let's think about this, Katie. It might work," Melanie said.

"It's out near Highway 89 but far from the road. No one would know you were even there," James said.

"This could work, Katie," Melanie said. "We could just clean it up and leave it like we found it."

"I don't know, Melanie," Katie said. "I will have to think about it. If my parents ever found out …"

"They won't," Melanie said.

"Do I get a big kiss for that, Melon Pops?" James said.

"Yes, you do, Peanut. Close your eyes," Melanie said, as she puckered up her lips. She planted a big kiss right on his forehead.

"No, that's not fair. I deserve more than that," James said. "See if I help you anymore."

Katie and Melanie chuckled at James's expense. They had a brief discussion about including Chase in their party plans and the hopes that Robbie and Gloria would be broken up by the time the party came around. Then they said their goodbyes, and Katie drove home.

After Katie's experience in that house, she was not pleased with her brother's idea to have their party there. She was praying for another great idea to come along so that the house would be removed from their options.

However, time passed quickly, and there were still no other options. Now all of her friends knew about the house on Highway 89 and expected it to be the party location. Katie decided to give in and set the date for the party. It would be on October 13 at 7:00 p.m. The location would be at 2148 Highway 89 in Salem, Massachusetts.

5 A FORESHADOWING OF EVENTS TO COME

The party date was set. Katie wondered if James could be trusted to keep quiet. She had never counted on him to do so with something that important. She had no choice at this point. She felt as though she owed him something for his silence. Only time would tell.

Katie had woken up that morning excited to attend school, knowing that she could daydream about Robbie and Chase during most of her classes. Nothing serious had developed between Chase and Melanie or between Chase and anyone else. That made Katie so happy. It almost gave her hope that something might happen for Chase and her.

She went down to the kitchen for breakfast, but no one was in the kitchen cooking this morning. The kitchen was dark, and there were no smells of eggs, bacon, or pancake syrup. That was out of the ordinary for her family. If her mother wasn't cooking, her father usually stepped in to do so. The stillness just didn't seem right to her. She was anxious to get to school, though. She was ready to daydream through most of her classes, so her day would pass quickly. Only her calculus class would not permit her any time for daydreaming. She grabbed a protein bar, yelled for James, and headed out the door.

Driving to school was less than typical. She waited at a stop sign while a woman, who was pushing a cart full of cans, crossed the street. *Do people really collect those?* she thought. She was caught behind the junior high's buses, which were lining up to take groups of eighth graders on a field trip. The last light before the turn into her school seemed unusually long, and of course, she had to park down the street from the school because the parking lot was full. By the time she made it to the front of the school to see her friends, the bell rang.

"Oh, I guess I will see you at lunch, love," Melanie said as she blew an air kiss to Katie and walked off to class.

"Later, Katie," said Jeb.

"Mwah! Much love, Kat. See you later," said Sandy as she jumped into Jeb's arms. He carried her across the threshold of the school while they laughed about it. They were such a fun and loving couple to be around. Only Jay had waited to actually say hello and walk into the building with Katie, until he had to go to a class in another hallway.

Katie hated days like this one, where she didn't have any time to joke around with her friends before school. These days always seemed to last longer, and that is not what she had been expecting.

First-through-third periods permitted her time to daydream. Today, she imagined being on the television show *Bachelor in Paradise*, with both Robbie and Chase fighting over her. She imagined that she was with Robbie, who was such a great kisser that she wanted to kiss him all the time, and so she did. He wrapped his towel around her waist and pulled her close to him. He softly touched her on her cheek and then ran his hand down her arm. He grabbed her by her buttocks and lifted her up to hold her as she wrapped her legs around his waist. Then he laid her down on her back, opened her towel, and pressed his leg between hers. Robbie kissed her on her neck. Then the bell rang.

It was time for second period. She continued to daydream as that class began. While her eyes were closed, Robbie continued to kiss her. His soft, light touches felt so good but sometimes, tickled too. When she giggled, he smiled so big. This beach did not have to be very big for them because they could have lain in that one spot forever, until in came Chase.

When he arrived, he was utter temptation. All of the women in Paradise had their eyes on him, and some of the men were envious of him. Chase scanned the women standing before him, but he was not impressed with what he saw. Katie stood up from the bed where she had been lying with Robbie and immediately caught Chase's attention. He called her to him. She came, and they danced to the music that was playing. It was romantic and passionate. After the dance, he pulled her tightly against him and kissed her. She laid her head on his shoulder and invited him to kiss down her neck and behind her ear. Then the bell rang.

It was time for third period. *I'm learning so much today,* she thought. At least, the day was passing quickly. She continued to daydream through third period. As Chase kissed behind her ear and down her neck, Robbie interrupted them. He wanted to challenge Chase for Katie's hand, but Chase told him that he had a date card and wanted to take Katie on a date.

The crowd was astonished. What would Katie decide to do? Would she take the date with Chase or stay with Robbie on the beach? Then it started to rain in her daydream. No, wait. That wasn't right. It was sunny and beautiful on the beach in her daydream. The sun was ripped from the sky of her daydream like a sheet of paper torn by claws. The rain poured from a gray sky. No, that isn't how Katie pictured it.

Everyone started chanting over and over, "Choose, Katie, choose!"

She yelled, "No! No, this isn't right!"

Lightning flashed. Thunder rolled. People on the beach began to crowd around her in zombielike fashion.

Next, she realized that she had stood up in class and was talking to the air. Her teacher asked her if she was okay. She realized that she had made a scene in class and went to the restroom. The whole day had been off since it had started.

By fourth period, she was ready to exchange texts with Chase. At least she could count on that. Still, she trembled at the thought of those daydreams. She thought that she must have fallen asleep. It was disturbing all the same. Then the bell rang.

It was fourth period. Since the day had not gone well so far, Katie wondered if fourth period was going to be what she needed to lift her spirits. She and Chase had gotten to the point where they were exchanging texts almost every day during fourth period. Katie loved the attention from him, even though they were only friends.

Chase was not in the room when she entered it, but that was common. In fact, Chase had served some time in detention for his tardiness. Unfortunately, today was another day that he did not make it to class before the bell rang. It was close, but Mr. Petrillo made sure he knew that he was not on time. The class chuckled a little. Chase was proud of his collection of tardy slips and wore them tucked inside the edge of his jeans, which had been an open invitation to pull on them for every girl on campus.

Once he was seated and settled, he looked over at Katie and smiled. She waited for that smile every day. That smile is what put a smile on her face for the rest of the day. But today was different. When he turned toward her, his eyes were solid black, and his lips were stitched closed. She shook her head and blinked her eyes. She looked again. Her eyes were playing tricks on her. There was that same beautiful smile she was used to seeing him wear every day. *It had been a crazy day,* she thought.

She didn't wait any longer to send her first text to him.

Well, does that tardy push you over the edge and back into the detention room again?

He responded.

Not yet! I think I have two more before I have to walk that hall of shame again. What about you? How many do you have? I know you're never tardy to this class, but what about your other classes? Detention is fun. LOL

She replied.

Tardy? Me? Never. You won't find me in there with you, babe. Sorry. I have things to do during lunch and after school like visit with my friends and oh yeah, homework. I'm a good student. :-)

"Chase and Katie, texting is not permitted in class,"

their teacher called out loudly. "Turn in your phones to me until the end of the day."

That cannot be possible, Katie thought. Petrillo never noticed when they were on their phones. They did this every day, and he never said a word. Both of them complied without argument because they knew that they were in violation of the classroom's rules. But how shocking and depressing it was. There would be no texting for the rest of the school day. Katie wished that she had stayed in bed. At least, it was lunchtime.

At lunch, Katie and her friends gathered in the cafeteria. Everything seemed to be going well, but Katie was just waiting for something strange or out of the ordinary to take place. The day was anything but typical for her.

She and Chase walked to the cafeteria together. That was something they usually did. Chase had begun to split his time in the cafeteria between the football players and Katie and crew. He ate with Katie and her friends and then went over to the football team during the last five-to-ten minutes of lunchtime.

Many of the football players who had friends outside of the football team did that, except for Jeb. Jeb stayed at our table with Sandy all the time. She was his number one priority. Football came second to her. Katie thought that was so sweet. He rarely took his eyes off Sandy when they were together.

The big news at the table was that no one would be

able to text Chase or Katie for the rest of the day due to their phones being confiscated by Petrillo. Chase was telling the story to the group before Katie had even dealt with the morning's experiences.

"Are you doing okay?" Jay asked.

"Yeah, it has just been a strange day," Katie said.

"Strange in what way?" he inquired.

"Have you ever been daydreaming, and the daydream doesn't turn out like you wanted it to?" Katie asked.

"Every time," Jay said and then laughed.

She playfully punched him. "Not like that," she said. "You lose control of the ending like in a dream or in a nightmare."

"I can't say that I have, Kat," he said. "That sounds really disturbing though, which takes me back to my original question. Are you okay?"

"No, I don't think I am," Katie said. "I don't think I am."

"Come here," Jay said and then put his arms around Katie.

She laid her head on his shoulder. He always made her feel so safe and secure. He was her best male friend. He was cute, strong, and had sandy-blond hair and blue eyes, which made him very attractive. His sense of humor left her laughing, even when she did not feel like doing so. His arms made her feel comforted, no matter what she feared. She could talk to him about anything and usually did. She could spend hours on the phone with him and never run out of something to say. She never worried about her hair or makeup in his presence because he had seen her at her best and worst.

Once, she had been sick with the flu for three weeks, and Jay hadn't even worried about catching it. He had climbed up the outside wall of her house so that he could get into her room to bring her favorite soup and lie with her in bed for a few laughs. Then he had gone out the window again. He was odd because he always used the window to come and go.

Katie's parents knew and loved Jay. They let him into Katie's room and weren't concerned. They knew that he and Katie were best friends and nothing more. They had been that way since they had met three years earlier.

The bell rang. Lunch was over. Now, Katie would have no communication with any of her friends for the rest of the day unless she passed them in the hallway. She never texted with them during her statistics class anyway because she really had to pay attention. That made the class pass quickly though. But she wondered if she could pay attention today. There were so many strange things happening that her mind was distracted. She wondered what else could possibly happen.

Her statistics class had been canceled. Her teacher had gone to a professional conference, so her class had been canceled for the day. Katie and her classmates were sent to the gym to be supervised by the coaches.

That's not bad at all, Katie thought. The coaches were sexy. The female students did not mind being supervised by them. Fifth period was making for a much better day so far. If it would only last through sixth and seventh period, Katie could see a complete turnaround of her day.

Evidently, other teachers were out that day too. Melanie had been assigned to the gym that period due to her teacher being absent also. Katie and Melanie loved watching Coach Ashby coach the girls' basketball team. Coach was so energetic, passionate, sweet, kind, and extremely competitive. He knew every student by name. He had a way of making every one of them feel special. His dark-brown eyes and hair, which fell into natural curls at his shoulders, melted every female student's heart. He was the definition of sexy.

Melanie was used to hollering at hot guys, so it did not surprise Katie that she found subtle ways to flirt with Coach Ashby without getting herself into too much trouble. Watching Melanie made the class period very entertaining for Katie, but she could not shake the feeling that she was being watched. In the large gymnasium of more than one hundred students, she hardly felt alone, but she felt like someone was standing in the shadows watching her and not wanting her to know that he was there. Then the bell rang.

Sixth period was when Katie usually took her naps. She was taking Art III. She was a great artist, but she could never draw under pressure. She had to be alone so that she could doodle what she wanted. Then she could draw. Her teacher understood that. As long as Katie completed her projects on time, Mr. Rye did not complain about her occasional naps during class. Katie was not the only student who had that problem but was the only one who made sure her projects were completed by their deadlines. Rye was not as understanding with others.

Katie laid her head down on her desk and fell fast asleep. Barely any time had passed before she started dreaming. She was in a dark room, which had a white candle in a holder. She was dressed all in white and was barefoot. She then walked on a red carpet down a hallway that appeared to be endless.

Soon, her feet and toes began sinking into the carpet. It turned into a narrow river of blood. She slowly sank into the river as red blood got all over her white dress, arms, hands, and face. She was reaching out for a book on a glass table when she awoke startled in a cold sweat. She decided that she must be getting sick. Then the bell rang.

During last period, Katie wasn't sure what she should do: Stay awake, daydream, or sleep. Since it was AP physics, she decided she would pay attention and participate in the class's activities. She usually participated in Mrs. Sykes's class. She wanted the concurrent college credit that she would receive if she made at least a B in the class.

Today as she participated in class, she could not shake the ominous feelings she had experienced from the moment that she had walked into an empty kitchen at home until now. She swore that she saw movement in the shadows of the darkened lab room behind her. Faces emerged from the shadows. None of her classmates seemed to see the people staring back at them from the lab room. There were little faces everywhere, and one big sinister presence was in the middle of them.

She finally got up and walked out of class. She went to the office to check out of school. Someone in the office retrieved her phone from Petrillo so that she could leave.

Katie went straight home and into her bedroom. Today was one of those days when she could draw. Her artwork showed a tall, dark figure with red eyes dressed in a robe and standing in the shadows of a physics lab with other little obscured faces looking out from behind it.

Over the next few weeks, she would continue to have these experiences and feelings throughout the day, but sharing them with Melanie and Jay made dealing with them much easier. They were so common that Katie became emboldened by them. She dived into her nightmares and daydreams and drew inspiration from them. She was learning from them and drawing strength from them.

This continued until one day when the nightmares and daydreams just stopped. As quickly as they had begun, they ended. There was no reasonable explanation why. She had no time for all that anyway. She had a party to plan.

6 THE PARTY BEGINS

Time passed quickly. Fall was in full force with its shades of red, orange, and brown leaves on the trees. October had arrived.

Melanie had done most of the planning for their first senior party of the year. Sandy and Melanie were supposed to be spending the night at Katie's house. Katie was supposed to be spending the night at Melanie's house. Chase had invited Robbie, which made things very interesting, especially since the rumor was that Robbie and Gloria had broken up. The guys were supposed to be having a guys' night at Jeb's house while Jeb was supposed to be staying at Jay's house.

Jeb was in charge of getting the alcohol for the party, which would be no problem for him. His house was filled with it, so no one would even miss what he took. Melanie and Sandy would bring the snacks, and Katie would bring the paper goods and cleaning supplies.

They were ready for the big night, except for Katie, who could still feel the cold air outside the basement door and fingers touching her spine as she stood in front of it. She just had to put that out of her mind, somehow. Besides, she had to be imagining that whole thing anyway, hadn't she? James had not seen anything when she had asked him. He had wandered through the entire house and had never spoken of anything weird or strange happening to him.

She decided to forget the whole thing and to have some fun with her friends at the party. She had other things to think about anyway. Both Chase and Robbie were going to be at this party. That meant that this might be the best party of the year.

Katie and Melanie decided that they should show up earlier than everyone else did to set things up and to figure out where their friends should park so that no one could see their cars from the road. They didn't have to worry about neighbors because the closest neighbor was about five miles up the road. They were isolated except for rare passersby on the highway.

The girls walked up to the house, and Katie used the key that she had taken from her mother's cabinet to open the door. Once they were inside, Katie and Melanie shouted and danced around with the biggest smiles on their faces.

The house was very big, so the girls decided to limit the rooms that they would use. The kitchen and living room was one open area, so they decided to utilize that space for food and general conversations. The house was furnished so that it could be used for an open house. They would have to be careful not to mess up the furniture.

Katie felt good about things, and she was ready for her guests to arrive. Everything was going to go well, no matter how creepy she may have felt over the last few weeks in the shadows of the rooms, how dark a room had seemed to be even with the lights on, and how cold the house had been even with the thermostat set on seventy-two degrees.

"Here are the last of the snacks," Melanie said as she walked past a door she had passed several times and not really noticed until then.

"Okay, great," Katie said. "Let's put them out on the counter."

"Katie, I felt a cold draft as I walked past that door," Melanie said. "It gave me chills and made my hair stand on end. I think we may need to adjust the thermostat."

Katie had a strange feeling as she stood there in the kitchen. She was a little light-headed and weak. She sat down on a kitchen stool for a minute. Just the mention of the word *colder* caught Katie's attention, but it was too late to cancel the party now and over what—a few irrational feelings? It was not going to happen. She refused to let it ruin her night. The cold draft meant nothing. She would adjust the thermostat again, and everything would be okay. Her thoughts were interrupted by a knock at the door.

Melanie answered the door. It was Sandy and Jeb. Melanie hugged them while also checking to make sure that Jeb's car was parked where it would not be seen from the road. She asked Jeb to go out and pull his car closer to the house to make room for the others. Katie hugged Sandy and asked her if it was too cold in the house. Sandy told her everything was perfect, including the temperature. Jeb ran in and grabbed Katie from behind, surprising her, and the antics began. They all laughed except for Katie, who could not seem to shake the feeling that the house was still too cold.

"Look what I found outside," Jeb said. Jay came in right behind Jeb, waved, and said his hellos. The girls welcomed him with hellos and hugs. Jeb and Jay went out to Jeb's car to bring in the alcohol.

"So what are you thinking about for tonight? Are you going for two girls or just one? Who will you pick?" Jeb joked.

"Ha ha! You're funny, my man," Jay replied. "I pick this pretty natural-blonde cheerleader. They're hard to find nowadays," he said and then laughed.

"Oh, I don't think so, bro. She's taken," Jeb said.

"Ah, but is she happily taken?" Jay said.

Both guys laughed, knowing their friendship was strong and that Sandy was head over heels for Jeb.

"Look at all of this booze. Doesn't your dad ever

miss any of this? We take it from him all the time," Jay said.

"Nope," Jeb said. "If I can't convince him that he must have broken the bottles in a drunken state, I convince him that he drank it and just doesn't remember it."

They laughed. They took the alcohol from the car and brought it into the kitchen. Then, they sat down in the living room to talk about sports.

Sandy set up the drinks' area and opened a bottle of Tequila. "At your service. Woohoo!" Sandy said as she poured drinks for everyone.

Someone rang the doorbell. Sandy and Melanie raced to answer it. It was Robbie and Gloria.

"Hey, I heard there was a big party goin' on here," Robbie said. "I hope you don't mind Gloria comin' along. We broke up, but we got back together in seventh period today. I just couldn't come without her." He kissed her on the lips. Melanie rolled her eyes.

"No, not at all," Sandy said, knowing Katie would be very disappointed. Melanie walked into the kitchen to let Katie know that Gloria was there with Robbie, but she was a second too late. Gloria was right behind Melanie. She wanted a bottle of alcohol to mix with the drink she already had. Katie took a long, deep breath and handed Gloria a bottle of whiskey. Gloria walked out of the kitchen to Robbie.

Katie turned to Melanie and said, "I thought they broke up."

Melanie responded, "They made up in seventh period today." Katie was beyond disappointed, especially since she knew that Melanie was just waiting to pounce on Chase.

The doorbell rang. Surprise, surprise, it was Chase, the only member of the party who had not yet arrived. There was no need for Katie to go to the door. Melanie was headed that way to greet him. Katie decided she would just lie low and serve snacks and drinks that night.

Melanie and Chase joined everyone else in the living area. They seemed to be comfortable with each other. Chase came to the counter to get himself a drink and to say hello to Katie.

"Great house," Chase said. "Perfect for our party."

"Yeah, it has worked out okay," Katie said.

"Can I get a drink?" Chase said.

"Sure. What do you want? Jeb got us everything," she said while smiling.

"I see that. I want a Jack-and-Coke. My dad drinks it and seems to like it," Chase said. "I don't really drink that much."

"Okay, a Jack-and-Coke coming right up," Katie said.

"Thanks! You know, you should do that more often," Chase said.

"Do what?" Katie asked.

"Smile," Chase replied. "You're very pretty when you smile."

Katie blushed a little at what he said. Then the two of them locked eyes for what seemed like a very long time before he went back to the group.

Katie continued to serve drinks as her friends continued to discuss football, other sports, and relationships. Then they began playing Truth or Dare. Participants either had to choose a question they had to answer truthfully or a task they were dared to complete. It was Chase's turn.

"What do you pick, Chase?" Sandy said.

"Dare," he replied.

"Lay a big kiss on the sexiest person in the room," Sandy said.

"Hmm, okay." He walked around the room for a minute. After building suspense over the person he would choose, he jumped on top of Jeb and planted a big kiss on him, telling him how incredibly sexy he was. Jeb pushed him away, and everyone laughed.

"Your turn, Jeb. Truth or dare?" Chase said.

"I'm going with truth," Jeb replied.

"Okay, truth. What are your true intentions for you and Sandy tonight?" Chase asked.

"Great question," Melanie said. "I'd really like to hear the answer to that one."

"Hey, I'm a man. I'm sorry, babe, but there is only

one thing on this man's mind. I must speak the truth," Jeb said.

"I wouldn't expect anything less from my man," Sandy said and then laughed along with her friends.

Katie continued to watch from the kitchen. Jay approached Katie and asked her why she was hanging out in the kitchen rather than hanging with the group. She responded, "I'm fine with serving drinks. Someone has to do it, right?"

Jay replied, "Yeah, that's the same reason I came over here."

"What do you mean?" Katie said.

"I'm a little sick to my stomach of watching Melanie and Chase flirting with each other," Jay said.

"What? You mean you have feelings for Melanie? Really? Why have you not told me this before now?" Katie said as she playfully punched him in the gut. "How long have you felt this way?"

"Shh, for a really long time," Jay said. "I've never even told Jeb. Don't say anything, okay? Just keep it to yourself."

"But how do you know she doesn't feel the same way about you if you don't ever tell her, Jay," Katie said.

"Has she ever mentioned having feelings for me?" Jay asked.

"No, but she …" Katie said.

"That's how I know," Jay interrupted. "I will just chill out with you if you don't care."

"That's fine," Katie replied.

Then Robbie and Gloria approached Katie and Jay in the kitchen. They asked for refills and wanted to know if it was okay for them to go upstairs for a little privacy. Katie nodded and reminded them not to mess up anything in the house. The rest of their friends cheered for Robbie as he led Gloria up the stairs.

Katie felt like someone had stepped on her heart. For three years, she had hoped for a chance to date Robbie, and he was going upstairs for privacy with his on-again-off-again girlfriend of three years. Jay grabbed Katie's hand.

"I guess it's not the end of the world," Katie said as she turned and hugged Jay. Chase was watching from the living room and came to the kitchen to break up their hug.

"What does a guy gotta do to get a drink around here?" he said. Katie stopped hugging Jay to get a drink for Chase.

"A guy needing a drink around here just has to get up and come pour it," Jay responded. There was a little tension in the moment, but it quickly passed when Katie said it was fine. Chase invited Katie and Jay to the living room to play games with the group. Katie and Jay decided to let people serve themselves and sat down in the living room to play with everyone else.

After a few more minutes of group games, Jeb suggested to Sandy that they go out to the pool. Sandy reminded him that she really did not like being around pools because she could not swim. He promised to be her life preserver and convinced her that she would be okay in the pool with a strong man like him. She gave in, and they walked down to the pool. The remainder of the group decided to play drinking games at Chase's suggestion.

The first drinking game was Never Have I Ever. In this game, participants state something they have never ever done. Those who have done it must take a shot of their choice of alcohol. Those who have not done it are safe.

"Never have I ever stolen a test from a teacher," Jay said. Chase took a drink.

"Never have I ever crushed on my PE coach," Chase said and then laughed as if he knew Melanie would have to take a drink, and she did. Katie also ended up having to drink.

"Never have I ever raised a hand to one of my parents," Melanie said. Jay took a drink. Melanie and Katie were very surprised at Jay's response. Jay had always been the calm, quiet, laid-back member of their group. He briefly explained that he had been defending his mom. They could tell that he didn't want to go into any more details about it.

Katie sat back and lost herself in her own thoughts for a few minutes. She was pleasantly surprised at how well the night was going despite her earlier feelings about the house and the whole Robbie-and-Gloria-and-Chase-and-Melanie thing. She sensed some positive vibes coming from the looks Chase gave her. She thought that he just might be more into her than he was into Melanie.

7 JEB AND SANDY FACE IT

Jeb and Sandy strolled playfully down the path to the pool. Jeb twirled Sandy in a circle a couple of times, pulled her in close, and touched her cheek with the back of his fingers. Sandy's steps were like watching a girl as she danced. Their love and affection for each other were rare among high school students. They had been in a relationship for two years, and they were one of the well-known couples in the high school.

Jeb was a defensive lineman on the football team, and Sandy cheered for him in the cheerleading squad. It was quite unusual for a couple like them to hang around with students like Katie, Jay, and Melanie, but Sandy had been friends with Jay and Melanie since second grade. She wasn't about to let cheerleading or Jeb change that. Jeb was okay with hanging out with the girls and Jay. Somehow, they just fit in together despite the norms of high school groups.

Jeb was an attractive guy of large build—five feet and eleven inches tall and nearly two hundred pounds. He had dark-brown hair with hazel-green eyes. His medium-tanned skin was the result of intentional exposure to the sun. Sandy was a sun worshipper, so he had to be one too if he planned to spend any time with her.

Jeb's family members had owned a butcher shop in town for over fifty years. They did very well for themselves but worked hard for what they had. Jeb and his brother would one day be expected to take over the family business, but that was not Jeb's dream. He dreamed of being an NFL defensive lineman. He wanted to go to college on a football scholarship and play football while he earned a degree in kinesiology.

Sandy was an attractive, young woman with a small frame and weighed about 110 pounds. She had beautiful naturally blonde hair and bright-blue eyes with medium-tanned skin. She was a dedicated member of the cheerleading squad and a loyal supporter of football and the football team.

Sandy came from the most modest means of all, not because her parents didn't make much money but because they had so many children in their home. Sandy was the second oldest of nine children. She loved little kids. She would give team stickers to them and paint their faces at the gates to every game. Her father was an insurance agent, and her mother was a stay-at-home mom. She had one goal in life right now. That was to follow Jeb to whatever college signed him on. She was in love with him. He was all that mattered to her.

As they reached the pool, Jeb stripped down to his underwear and then quickly dived in. He commented about the chill of the water due to the time of the year. Sandy sat by the edge of the pool. She was afraid to get into the water.

Jeb swam over to her and kissed her lovingly. Then he pulled her top off. Right afterward, he splashed her with water, and she screamed because of the cold temperature. She was sure that her screams and their fun foreplay activities could be heard by the others in the house.

"Baby, don't you know you can trust me?" Jeb said. "Come on into the pool. I will carry you around."

"Yes, I know I can trust you," Sandy said, "but you must promise not to let go of me unless I tell you it's okay. Promise?"

"Of course, baby," Jeb said.

"Promise!" Sandy said. For the first time, Sandy was able to make Jeb understand how afraid she was of the water.

"I promise," Jeb said. He kissed her on the forehead.

She stood up and slipped off her shorts. She sat back down on the side of the pool. Jeb scooped her up into his arms so that he could carry her around the three-foot end of the pool while they talked and laughed.

After a while, Jeb asked Sandy if she wanted to learn how to float on the water. "Okay," she said, "but keep your hands on me." Jeb promised he would. He told her to lie back on the water while he supported her weight with his hands. She kept one leg on the bottom of the pool for a little bit as she struggled with her fear of the water and her trust of Jeb. Both feelings were very strong and powerful.

Finally, she lifted her leg. She was almost floating on top of the water. Jeb's hands were firmly underneath her as support for her back. She could start to feel her own body being lifted from his hands and supported on top of the water. She still insisted that he not remove his hands. She was excited and laughing, which caused her to start to sink at one point. Jeb quickly grabbed her, and then she was firm and steady once again.

The trust had been established. Now Sandy felt like she could do more. She wasn't exactly ready to learn how to swim, but she wanted Jeb to get her ready to float and then let go of her. She was nervous yet thrilled. She was finally going to overcome her fear of the water. Sandy lay on her back on top of the water supported by Jeb's hands. Soon, Jeb only had his fingertips under her back.

Sandy was floating on the water. Her eyes were closed, and she was taking in the night air. She could feel soft fingertips on her spine where Jeb's hands were touching her. With her eyes still closed, she whispered to Jeb, "Thank you, Jeb. You don't know what this means to me. I promise it's okay to completely let go of me now."

"Sandy, what did you say? You've floated away from me," Jeb said. "Keep floatin'. I'm comin' to you." He started to swim toward her and hit a solid wall of water that was impassable and impenetrable.

When Sandy realized that Jeb was not still touching her but something else was, she panicked. Something pulled her midsection straight down underneath the water. She struggled, but something was holding her under the water and curling Itself around her as if It were embracing her. She tried to see what It was, but all she could do was struggle for air. She was too desperate to breathe to see It.

Finally, It let her up for air, and then a second later, It fiercely pulled her back under the water, as if to say, "I am not done with you yet." She barely had a second to scream before she was back under the water again. The others heard her scream but thought nothing of it. They thought that it was just Jeb and Sandy playing in the pool.

Then just as she felt she could not fight anymore, something in the water stared into her face. It took on a mirror image of her. It looked at her while she was running out of air. It tilted Its head to the right, leaned in closely, and watched as the life left her body. Then It took her body forcefully. Hands made of water wrapped around her neck, pulled her up out of the water, and snapped her neck in front of Jeb. It swung her lifeless body in the air violently before dropping it into the pool.

Jeb yelled, but the noise in the house had become so loud, they couldn't hear him. They had turned on some music and were dancing in the living room. Robbie and Gloria had even come back downstairs and had joined the group as they had heard the music playing and had decided to join the dancing.

Jeb had tried everything he could to get to her, but he was met with a solid wall of water at every attempt. He couldn't push, swim, dive, or go around the wall. He couldn't even get out of the pool because he was walled in on all four sides. Finally, the walls of water collapsed around him. Jeb couldn't believe what he had just seen. He went over to Sandy's lifeless body in the deep end of the pool. All he wanted to do was hold her.

After holding Sandy's body for a minute, he felt movement. He thought that what he had seen had been some sort of hallucination. He tried to get Sandy's attention. Suddenly, Sandy's head turned backward so her face stared up at his, and a deep voice said, "You're next." She let out a deep and sinister laugh that frightened Jeb back to his senses.

He let go of her body, raced to get out of the pool, and went up the path toward the house. About halfway up the path, Jeb felt a powerful force pulling him backward. A hand that had been formed from the water in the pool had grabbed hold of him. It dragged him across the concrete and back into the pool. He heard Sandy's voice asking him, "Don't you want to swim, Jeb, or do you just prefer to work instead?"

The voice went on to talk about how he had worked for his father's butcher shop since he had been eight years old and had played with meat hooks as his toys. The hand pulled his body twenty feet upward and left him dangling in the air from its fingertips. No one saw or heard him in his distress. Finally, the hand thrust his body into the pool and then into the side of a nearby shed. Barely breathing and conscious, Jeb made an effort to get up and go inside the house.

While heading toward the front of the house, the shed's doors flew open, and Jeb heard something dragging across the ground. He had nearly made it to the cars when the object that had been dragging along the ground caught him right between the shoulder blades and made three separate thrusts deeper into his flesh. A dark figure in the form of a man and dressed as a butcher placed his body on a hanging meat hook. It pushed his body down onto the meat hook with force. It began to talk to Jeb in a multitude of male and female voices, changing frequently. Jeb recognized none of them.

"Do you remember being nine years old and seeing that meat hook on the floor of your father's butchery?"

It said. "You watched the men as they dug that hook into the slabs of meat that were brought into the shop every day. You cursed the day that your father told you that you would have to learn to use the meat hook to move, lift, and hang the meat. You swore you would never do it."

"Even though you learned to use it and have been hanging meat on it while working for your father these past five years, the fear of having a meat hook stuck in your own flesh has haunted your nightmares. Bone-cracking, flesh-tearing, blood-dripping, and pain-throbbing meat hooks!"

The dark figure now formed the shape of a person that had a devil-like head with horns. Its hands had claws with extralong, sharp, pointed nails. It dipped Its pointed nails into Jeb's dripping blood and tasted it. "Yes, I taste fear," It said. Then It looked deep into Jeb's eyes as he kicked and yelled with what little strength he had left.

"I can see into your soul, Jeb. There is much darkness to be found there, especially now." It laughed.

Then It broke open Jeb's body by pulling forward and inward on both of his shoulders, leaving Jeb's spine fully exposed. Just before It dropped his body to the ground in front of the shed, It dug Its claws deep into Jeb's broken body.

"Yes, another captured, empty soul," It said. Then, It just disappeared.

8 THE EVENING'S PRELUDE

Everything was quiet outside after that. The water in the pool was still, even though Sandy's body was floating in it. The night was lit by a nearly full moon. The sound of crickets was all that could be heard. Jeb's body lay in the shadows just beside the shed.

In the house, music was playing, and everyone was dancing and enjoying snacks and drinks. Everyone seemed to be having a great time. Katie couldn't be more pleased with how things were going. If she only knew what had just happened and what was still to come.

"Okay, Katie. Watch and learn," Melanie said. Katie observed Melanie attempting to get closer to Chase by playing a slow song and trying to get him to dance. Robbie and Gloria were already dancing. Melanie reached out, took Chase's arm, and invited him to dance with her.

After a slight glance toward Katie, he accepted her offer. He talked and danced with Melanie through the first song. Katie knew that Jay had seen Chase's glance. She knew that it would not get past him. Jay was good at reading people. She knew she would not be able to hide the emotional effect that those slight glances in her direction had on her.

"So it looks like I'm not the only one hiding feelings tonight," Jay said.

"What do you mean? Is it that noticeable?" Katie asked.

"I don't know if anyone else noticed it, but I did. I noticed that look he gave you too," Jay said. "Come on, Katie. Dance with me."

Katie reluctantly agreed to dance with Jay. Shortly after he asked her to dance with him, he interrupted their dance by breaking in on Melanie and Chase. "May I cut in?" Jay said.

Chase backed away from Melanie as if to say yes and then turned toward Katie and held out his hand as if to ask her to dance. She accepted his offer. Katie was now dancing with Chase—a guy who just might be the best-looking guy in their high school. Slow dancing was going great for them. Katie could tell that even Melanie enjoyed her dance with Jay.

"So you look like you're having a really good time tonight," Jay said.

"I really am. How about you? Are you having a good time?" Melanie asked.

"Yeah, oh yeah," Jay said, "even better now that I got a chance to dance with you."

"Aw, you're so sweet, Jay." She kissed him on the cheek. He moved in a little closer and held her a little tighter. He was just enjoying this chance to hold her for a few dances. Katie and Chase were enjoying their first dance too.

"It looks like everyone is having a great time," Chase said.

"I agree. I think things have gone well," Katie said.

"Are you having a good time?" Chase asked.

"Yeah, I am," she replied and then laid her head on his shoulder. Chase laid his head against hers and closed his eyes.

Katie noticed Melanie was becoming uncomfortable with how long she had been dancing with Chase. She could see that Melanie was intensely watching the interaction between Chase and her. She was putting more and more distance between Jay and herself. Katie knew it was time for her to stop dancing with Chase. After a couple of dances, Melanie decided to cut in. Jay walked over, took Katie by the hand, and put his arm around her. She looked up at him, and they smiled at each other.

"May I have this dance?" Katie asked Jay, who graciously accepted her offer. Jay had always been such a good friend to Katie. They had been friends since she moved to Salem, which is why they said, "Ew," or laughed when anyone suggested that they should date or that they might make a great couple. Tonight, everyone could see how they were such great friends to each other.

Suddenly, the music came to a stop. "I have an idea," Robbie said. "Yo, let's play hide-and-seek." The others groaned. "No, look. This house is really old," he said. "You never know what secrets it holds."

"My mom is going to have an open house here in about two weeks," Katie said. "We really can't—"

"Aw, c'mon Katie," Chase said. "It would be fun. There is no telling what we would find."

"Chase, will you team up with me?" Melanie said.

Chase hesitated for just a moment and glanced at Katie, who was looking down. "Sure," he responded.

"It's you and me, kid," Jay said to Katie as he winked at her.

"What has happened to Jeb and Sandy?" Melanie asked. "They appear to have gotten out of the pool and disappeared to somewhere."

"Everyone keep an eye out for them while we're playing," Katie said. "All of you can hide first. Jay and I will be the seekers."

"Count to a hundred," Robbie said.

Robbie and Gloria went in one direction, and Chase and Melanie went in another direction. Katie and Jay sat down on the floor. They counted together. After reaching the number thirty, they stopped counting and started talking.

"They should be far enough away now that we don't have to keep counting," Jay said.

"Sorry that you didn't get to go with Melanie," Katie said.

"Eh, it's okay. Sorry that you didn't get to go with Chase," Jay said. Katie started giggling.

"Yep, I knew it," Jay said. "You're really into him. Damn, this sucks for both of us tonight." Jay stood up. He extended his hand to help Katie get up.

"Yeah, no need to remind me," Katie said, "but I have you, and that's pretty fabulous."

"Pretty fabulous, huh?" Jay said.

"Yep! Pretty fabulous," Katie said as she took his arm and they started down the hall.

9 IT ATTACKS AGAIN

Robbie and Gloria had spent the last three years in an on-again-off-again relationship. They were the most popular students in school, and rightly so, since they held the most desired positions on campus as quarterback and captain of the cheerleading squad.

Robbie was a down-to-earth guy and never let his position go to his head. He socialized with different groups at the high school. Many different types of people referred to him as a friend.

Gloria was a little more selective about the people she socialized with. She was usually only seen around the other cheerleaders at the school. Hanging out with Robbie took her out of that element and forced her to socialize in other circles. When she was in those other circles, she could hold her own in a conversation.

Besides their obvious athletic abilities and talents, they were very attractive people as well. Robbie had dark-brown hair and eyes, nicely tanned skin, and a gorgeous smile with perfect pearl-white teeth that caught every girl's attention. He stood about five feet, ten inches tall and weighed about 175 pounds, which was solid muscle.

He never went anywhere without his letterman's jacket. He was very loyal to his teammates and friends but not quite so loyal to his girlfriend, which caused a few of their breakups over the years. His family was slightly better off than a typical family of middle income, but Robbie carried himself as though he had $1 million in his pocket. He also dreamt of being in the NFL.

Gloria had dark-brown hair and eyes, beautifully bronzed skin, and a smile that made even those who wanted to dislike her find a way to like her. She stood about five feet, seven inches tall and weighed about 120 pounds.

She was a real advocate for the football team and other high school sports. She was very loyal to the school administration, coaches, and her squad, but the loyalty ended there, which had caused the other half of her breakups with Robbie over the last three years. She came from a family of modest, middle-income means. Her family life was filled with rich cultural traditions and celebrations.

Gloria's mother passed away when Gloria was very

young, so she did not remember very much about her mother. All of her memories of her were very sweet and loving. Her relationship with her stepmother had been anything but that. Her stepmother, Cinthia, had made no effort to try to have a relationship with Gloria. She had her own children, who were being well cared for by Gloria's father, and that was all that mattered to her.

Gloria's stepmother had always been critical of her. Cinthia had left her without a mother figure in her life. Gloria had always been afraid to stand up to her stepmother for the way she treated her, primarily because she had been taught better than that. The truth was that Gloria did not really have a disrespectful bone in her body, and her stepmother knew and took advantage of it.

Gloria dreamed of going straight from high school into college for another four years. She planned on living high school over and over again by teaching athletics and cheerleading at the high school level after college graduation.

"Now we can return to that room we were in earlier tonight," Robbie said.

"This is so exciting—a little creepy in this old house—but still exciting," Gloria said.

They walked upstairs and entered the first bedroom on the right side of the hall. A cool breeze blew into the room from the window, which had been left wide open. It gave them chills, so Robbie quickly walked across the room to close it. When he did, he thought he saw something move across the floor, so he stumbled as if to avoid stepping on it.

"What was it?" Gloria asked.

Robbie closed the window and locked it. Then he looked around the floor and found nothing there. He turned his attention to Gloria. "It was nothing. Forget it. We've more important things to think about," Robbie said. He grabbed Gloria by the waist and pulled her close to him. He ran his hands along her back and waist. She moved her hand down his abdomen and then used her arms to pull him closer to her.

Gloria pressed herself against him and lifted her right leg to wrap it around him at the thigh. He grabbed her leg and proceeded to kiss her neck and chest. He opened her blouse. She closed her eyes and dropped her head backward to enable him to embrace her fully. He picked her up, and she wrapped both legs around him.

He sat down on the end of the bed with her on top of him. She removed his shirt and slid her hands down his arms and across his well-developed muscles. He was solid. Just feeling how ripped his arms and chest were aroused her. She playfully hiked her skirt. He grasped her by the thighs. She unbuttoned his jeans and slid her hand around his back and just under his waistband. He brushed his cheek against her breast and kissed her abdomen lightly. She leaned into him. She whispered to him, and he encouraged her with sweet words.

"I love you, baby," he said. "You're my world."

Whispering, she replied, "I love you too, Robbie."

They kissed passionately. They gazed into each other's eyes. Gloria sat up to share something with Robbie when suddenly something moved in the room and caught her attention.

"Holy shit!" she said as she climbed off the bed and moved to the opposite wall from where she had seen the unknown object show Itself and disappear. All she knew for sure was that It had red eyes. She backed herself up to the wall and was extremely frightened.

"Baby, are you okay?" Robbie said. "What the hell happened?" He looked over at her and saw how frightened she was. He went to her side.

"Hey! Hey, what's wrong?" Robbie said. "What is it?" He reached out to take her hand and comfort her. He stepped in front of her, blocking the view of where she had been staring.

She quickly shifted so that she could see around him. She cocked her head to the side, looking around Robbie. She was unable to utter a sound at that point.

Robbie looked into her eyes and got closer to her face. He tilted his head to mimic her. Finally, he realized she was fixated on something behind him. He turned his head to see what it was. He saw nothing. He waved his hand in front of her. He tried to pinpoint exactly where she was looking. He walked to the other side of the bed, closer to where he had seen something earlier. Robbie still had no idea what had happened. He attempted to pick Gloria up and carry her out of the room, but she violently resisted his attempts to move her.

"Gloria, what is the matter with you?" he yelled. He finally caught her attention. Her eyes moved from where she had been staring to Robbie. She pointed at the wall in front of them. He looked around.

"What is it, Gloria?" Robbie said. "What is it?"

"It was there, and then it was gone," Gloria struggled to say.

Robbie grasped her face in his hand, forcing her to look at him. "What was there?" he said.

Visibly frightened, she responded, "I don't know. It just had red eyes."

"What had red eyes? Talk to me, Gloria," Robbie said.

"I don't know!" she yelled back at him. "It was like a bat or a really large bug, but it had red eyes."

"That doesn't make any sense, Gloria," Robbie said. "I've looked around, and there's nothing here."

"Whatever I saw was real, and it had red eyes," Gloria insisted. "I can't explain how it just disappeared."

She stood facing Robbie. She was looking above him and once again, had become speechless. Robbie looked above him and saw nothing. He asked her what was wrong, but she had difficulty trying to form her words. She said the word *spider* with a nervous, shaky voice. The word was broken into distinct sounds and syllables. Robbie realized what she was saying, and he reacted.

Knowing Gloria was terrified of spiders, he began to search for the spider in the area in which she was looking. He followed her eyes to the ceiling over his head, but he still did not see anything. Now her eyes were looking directly above his head. She was pointing right at him. He started to swat above his head and patted his hair. "Is it on me?" he asked.

She managed to shake her head nervously. The one spider that had creeped down toward Robbie's head now reached the floor. It was headed slowly toward Gloria. The spider was not what had her so jittery and nervous. She now saw hundreds of spiders pouring into the room from every crevice. She jumped from the floor onto the bed. Robbie saw the first spider on the floor. He went to step on it, and it moved. Gloria screamed as the spiders climbed all over her, from her head to her toes. She heard Robbie trying to reassure her that he was going to kill the spider so that she could calm down. She remained on the bed but backed up against the wall.

In a muffled voice, she cried out for his help. "Help me, Robbie," she said. Her voice was barely audible.

"I'm not going to let it get you, Gloria," he said.

She watched him search for the first large spider as many smaller spiders continued to smother her and bind her to the wall with their webbing. She was struggling to breathe.

Why were these spiders attacking her? It knew how much she feared spiders. That's why! She didn't only fear spiders. She had one other fear, which It would take advantage of just minutes before she stopped breathing. It assumed the appearance of her stepmother, only she was dark and dreary, and her eyes were charcoal black as if they had been burned that way. It looked deep into Gloria's eyes and spoke to her with her stepmother's voice.

"You know better than to leave the house to be with that boy. What makes you think any boy would want you? You have ragged hair and the face of a boy. There is only one thing a boy would want from you—sex! You probably give it away like candy.

"Why, your own mother would rather be dead than be around you? You were too ugly even for her to want, and now, I'm stuck with you. Your father never has time for anyone in this family because he doesn't like his fat and ugly daughter. You are a nasty, filthy child. You are lucky for each and every day that I let you live," It said. "Speaking of that, time's up. Go be with your mommy in hell."

Then It laughed like a wicked woman causing a tear to form in the corner of Gloria's eye. Within seconds, the spiders began biting her all over her body. She experienced excruciating pain from the number of bites that she received all at once. Finally, the spiders poured down her throat. She choked, gagged, and breathed her last breath.

Robbie continued to chase that one big spider until he could no longer find it. He had torn the bedroom apart looking for it. Finally, he turned his attention toward Gloria, who was flat against the wall just above the edge of the bed. He fell to the floor in complete shock. He could not believe what he was seeing. He called out her name. He knew that he needed to get her down if she was going to be okay. He ran to the bedroom door, opened it, and called out for help.

Katie thought she heard some screams coming from upstairs, so Katie and Jay quickly went in that direction. "Those yells were loud. I think they are ready to quit or at least change seekers," Katie said. She and Jay laughed.

As they reached the landing of the second floor, they became very quiet. They expected to discover their friends around the corner. When they reached the first bedroom, they were shocked by what they saw.

Katie's hand moved to cover her mouth as her chin dropped. Robbie was walking around and making strange jerky movements, as if chasing something small and unseen. They could barely see Gloria, who was underneath what appeared to be stretched cotton, which was so thick that it had bound her to the wall. What could have done this? How was this possible?

10 A TANGLED WEB IS WOVEN

"What the hell is going on in here?" Katie asked. She shook her head in disbelief.

"I don't know, Katie," Robbie said hysterically. "I don't know. Please help her."

"What is that all over her?" Katie said. Katie stared at Gloria as tears filled Katie's eyes.

"I'm not really sure," he said.

"What the hell is that, Robbie?" Jay said.

"I don't know. I think … I think it's webbing from a spider," Robbie replied. There was disbelief in his voice. Even though he had been in the room, he could not explain what had taken place.

"No, that's fuckin' crazy, dude," Jay said, slamming his fist into the wall. "You're the only person who was in here with her," Jay said in an accusatory tone. Jay looked in Robbie's direction, believing that he must have had something to do with it.

"What are you tryin' to say?" Robbie asked as he pushed Jay.

"There is no tryin' to say it. I said it," Jay replied as he pushed Robbie back.

Katie stepped between them and yelled, "Stop it! What is wrong with you two? She is dead, no matter how it happened. It doesn't look like anything Robbie could've done, Jay. Now stop this, please."

"Are we cool?" Robbie asked Jay. "I wanna get her down and get this stuff off her now, dude."

"Yeah, we're cool," Jay said. He hesitated for a few moments.

Robbie and Jay removed her from the wall. Katie and Robbie pulled at the webbing to uncover Gloria's body. While removing the webbing, Katie noticed a few small spiders coming out of Gloria's mouth. She leaned over Gloria's mouth and opened it with her fingers. Hundreds of spiders poured out onto her body. Katie backed away quickly. Her movement startled Robbie and Jay, who were not able to see what she saw. She was breathing heavily.

When Robbie asked her what she had seen, she just responded that she had seen nothing. Robbie told Katie that he did not believe her and kept his distance from Gloria after that.

Jay suggested they stay away from Gloria's body since

they were unsure if the spider that bit her was poisonous. Jay looked over at Robbie. Robbie was extremely afraid. What did Robbie know about Gloria's death? What was he hiding?

"We need to get the hell out of here," Robbie said.

"What are you talking about? We need to call the police," Katie said. "Something we can't explain has happened to Gloria."

"I knew she was afraid of spiders, but she wasn't like allergic or anything," Robbie said. "A spider shouldn't have done this to her!" He said loudly and hysterically.

"Just calm down. We don't even know what kind of spider it was," Jay said. "Some poisonous spiders can kill you with only one bite. They're very rare around here, but anything is possible, especially in this house."

"Does anyone have their phone? We need to call our parents, her parents, an ambulance, the hospital, the pol—," Katie said.

"No, no, no, and no! Not from here, you're not!" Robbie said. "We lost cellular connection about three miles up the road from here. I'll go get in my car, drive down the road, and call them."

"Wait! Why are you the one going? Why not Katie or me?" Jay asked curiously.

"Are we gonna have a problem again, Jay?" Robbie asked.

"Just wondering why it's you," Jay replied.

Katie told Robbie that there wasn't a problem and

sent him to go make the call for help. He went down the stairs and out the door. By the time he reached his car, his phone was ringing. But that was impossible! Cellular service was not available in that area.

He was surprised but grateful when he saw that it was his mother. She was calling to find out what time he would be home in the morning. He proceeded to tell her everything that had happened, where they were, the people he was with, and how they needed help for Gloria. She agreed to contact the police to get help for them immediately and told him that she was on her way. She told him to tell his friends that they needed to call their parents too. He agreed to do so. As he hung up, he heard laughter coming from a nearby basement window.

"Chase? Melanie? Chase, is that you? Damn it, Chase, is that you?" Robbie continued to follow the sound of laughter until it led him to the sliding glass doors at the back of the house. He went inside the house.

He decided to go to the basement door near the kitchen. He felt a cold chill as he stood outside that door. He opened it and yelled into the basement. No one responded. He told them that the game was over. No one responded. He heard more laughter, reached for the light, and turned it on. He decided that he had to go into the basement if he wanted to find Chase and Melanie and tell them what was going on.

Meanwhile, Katie was crying and holding Gloria's

head and shoulders in her lap. "I don't understand what has happened," Katie said. "One minute we're all playing games, and the next, we're up here and this happens."

Jay moved to sit beside Katie. He put his arm around her and pulled her toward him. "I'm sorry, Katie," he said. "I guess I'm not actually being much help to you either."

Katie turned on him and said, "No, you aren't. What did you mean earlier when you said, 'especially in this house'? If there is something I should know, shouldn't you tell me?" she asked tearfully.

"It's nothing. Just forget it," he said.

"Where is everyone? We need to find Chase, Melanie, Jeb, and Sandy," Katie said.

"Okay, I will go look for them and come right back once I find them," he stated.

"No! You're not leaving me in here all alone with … no!" she responded.

"Okay, you go look for everyone, and I will stay here with Gloria," he suggested.

"Never mind, I don't want to be alone in here or out there. Maybe, we could just make a lot of noise so they could hear us," she suggested.

"That might work," he replied.

They decided to yell that the game was over and that everyone needed to come out of hiding. They yelled about how important it was and called it an emergency. Chase and Melanie, who had been hiding in the laundry room of the house, began laughing.

"Yeah, right! Like we would really fall for that one," Melanie said.

"We've listened to them search upstairs the whole time and never even check the downstairs. They sure give in easily," Chase said.

"Back to what you were saying about my eyes," she said. Melanie tossed her hair back and invited his every compliment.

"Huh, well, they are very pretty. You're very pretty," he said.

"Thank you."

Chase leaned in and kissed her. She returned his kiss as he boosted her up on top of the dryer. They continued kissing each other until the dryer clicked on. They both started laughing and accused each other of pressing the button.

While kissing her on the neck, Chase said, "It's okay for you to admit it. You pressed it. You're just a little freaky." They continued laughing.

"Me? You're the one being a little freaky," she said. "I'm just not sure how you were able to get your hand over there to press the button and then back on me so quickly." There was more laughter.

"That's because I didn't press the button," he said with a slight chuckle.

"I didn't press the button either," she said, getting more serious about the matter.

They stopped kissing and looked at each other. They were a little spooked by the whole thing. Melanie got down from the dryer, and both of them moved toward the laundry room door. As they reached the door, the dryer stopped. Because they were spooked, both of them decided to go outside to hide instead. They slipped out the back door, even though they heard the calls for help from Jay and Katie. They believed that their cries were part of the game.

They went around the back of the house toward the pool and decided to continue their flirtatious behaviors while hiding behind some bushes.

"I must admit that I've liked having all of this time with you tonight," she said.

"Yeah, it's been nice," he said as he leaned in to begin kissing her neck once again. "You're as sweet as you are beautiful."

"Okay, lover boy, enough of that," Melanie said. "Isn't it odd that we haven't come across any of the others? You would think that we would have at least seen Jeb and Sandy out here near the pool. They have been off somewhere alone for over an hour now."

"Maybe we should go find a place where we can comfortably be alone for a little while," he said. "We could go hide around the side of the house where my car is parked."

"Well, we could do that," she said as she ran her finger playfully down the front of his shirt, "but I think we should suggest a new game and save some of that for later when it's time to crawl into a bed upstairs." She smiled really big at him, knowing she had piqued his interest for later that night, and then she walked away.

He replied while following her, "I like the way you think."

"So shall we go check on the others starting with Jay and Katie, who are still yelling upstairs?" Melanie asked. They both laughed.

"That's a good place to start," Chase said. "I think if we continue around this way, we will come to the pool and the pathway to the sliding glass doors that go into the living room." He led her around the bushes toward the pathway.

As they got to the end of the pathway, Melanie noticed that the pool was covered, except for one corner of it. Since she knew Jeb and Sandy had gone to swim in it earlier, she found this very odd. Melanie got closer to the pool and started to pull the cover from it. She noticed something floating under it. She told Chase and got into the pool.

As she went under the water to swim to the floating object, the water darkened so much that she could not see the object anymore. The pool cover started to coil around her. As she tried to swim up to the top of the water, she felt it weighing her down. She felt as though she was unable to get loose.

She also felt something swimming around her legs, but she could not see anything. Things were moving about in the water around her. She felt hands touching her but still could not see anything. She struggled fiercely, and in doing so, the cover only seemed to get tighter.

Finally, she saw the object that was floating in the pool. She reached for it and grabbed the side of it. It flipped sideways, and the face of Sandy turned directly toward her. Melanie was stunned to see the skeletal face of her dear friend. She pushed her away.

While moving backward, she was relieved to find Sandy swimming in the pool behind her. Melanie thought she looked beautiful under the water and almost angelic.

Melanie attempted to go up for air, but Sandy pulled her back down. She signaled to Sandy that she needed to go up for air, but again, Sandy pulled her back down. The pool cover began wrapping around Melanie again as Sandy grabbed onto her, hugging her. She tried to push away from Sandy, but Sandy had a strong hold on her. Forcibly, Melanie pushed away from her. Sandy's eyes turned blood red, her mouth became an open, black hole, and her face turned pale white.

After a brief struggle, Sandy let go of Melanie. Melanie was then able to make it to the surface, where she found that Chase had pulled the cover off the pool and had discovered Sandy's body. Chase had pulled Sandy from the water.

Melanie got out of the water and yelled at Chase. "Stop! Get away from her, Chase!" Melanie said in a frightened tone as she climbed from the pool.

"What? Why? It's Sandy. She's not breathing," Chase responded in a heightened state of emergency.

Melanie cautiously approached Chase and Sandy's body. She peered over Chase's shoulder to look at Sandy's face. It was Sandy. She was just her simple, beautiful self but paler and slightly bluer. "That's not possible. She was just swimming with me in the pool," Melanie said frantically as she shook.

"She wasn't swimming in the pool with you," Chase said. "She has been floating in the pool for a while now. The big question is where is Jeb? He promised not to let go of her in the pool. I don't see him anywhere."

"I don't understand," Melanie said slowly. "Sandy was swimming with me in that water, and the pool cover wrapped around me and nearly drowned me."

"Melanie, that's just not possible. Sandy is dead, and I removed the pool cover when you jumped in."

Melanie thought, *what happened to me? What did I just experience? Was it just my imagination?* Suddenly, she felt chills running up and down her spine. She felt a presence behind her, but she was afraid to look over her shoulder. She bent down next to Chase and whispered to him. She asked him if there was anyone behind her. She watched as his eyes became very big. She knew that something was there. She jumped up and turned around quickly, as if to strike something. Nothing was there.

"What are you doing?" Chase said.

"Something was behind me. I saw it in your eyes. Your eyes got really big when I questioned you. I felt Its presence," she told him.

"What are you talking about?" Chase said. "I was just noticing that Jay is yelling at us from the window. They've been trying for about fifteen minutes to get our attention. Sandy's dead body in the pool could be why."

"That's right! They have been," she said. She looked up at Jay in the window. She wiped away her tears and tried to pull herself together. "We need to find Jeb. He's gotta be responsible for this," she said in an angry tone.

"Now wait a minute. We don't know what happened here," Chase said. "We need to get everyone together first."

Melanie wasn't convinced of that. She took a deep breath and exhaled. Chase picked up Sandy's body and started carrying it to the house. Melanie walked alongside him. They walked around the pool on the side near the tool shed. Melanie noticed that Chase moved over awkwardly to block her view of the shed as they passed it. She could barely see the dents on the shed as they went by it. Chase worried that something horrible may have happened to Jeb.

They went into the house, and Chase placed Sandy's body on the couch in the living room. Melanie grabbed her cell phone from the counter and tried to get service. She had no luck. They heard sounds coming from the door to the basement.

"Melanie, go upstairs," Chase said.

"Not without you," she replied.

"Go. I'm just going to brace the door to the basement and make sure the other doors down here are locked," he insisted.

"I will wait right here for you then," she said firmly.

The house seemed eerily quiet while Chase went to lock the doors. She couldn't even hear Jay and Katie anymore. Sandy's body twitched. That caught Melanie's attention. Melanie began to shake. She said, "Sandy?" but there was no reply.

She heard bones cracking and saw Sandy's limbs bending in ways that they shouldn't naturally bend. The whole room turned white. Suddenly, blood began dripping from the tops of the walls. She heard Sandy say, "Melanie, help me. It hurts, Melanie. It hurts so bad here." The more It talked, the more the voice changed from Sandy's voice to a deeper male voice. Then Sandy stood up and bent sideways. Her body moved in the most unnatural ways. Sandy moved toward Melanie. Melanie stood in utter fear, shaking.

Then Chase grabbed her by the shoulder. She screamed. She hugged Chase as she watched Sandy slowly walk back to her place on the couch and the room return to normal.

"Get me out of here, please," she said.

"What do you mean? C'mon let's go upstairs," Chase said. Chase had put a chair against the basement door and had locked the sliding glass doors, the front door, and the side door.

"No. Let's just go. Please, let's just get out of here," Melanie begged.

"Melanie, we're going upstairs. C'mon," Chase said as he started up the stairs. After one glance around the room, Melanie quickly followed him.

"Chase! Melanie! We've been calling for everyone," Jay said.

"Yeah, we know," Chase said.

"We heard you. We're sorry. We thought it was part of the game," Melanie said.

"What is wrong with Sandy? We saw you carrying her," Katie said.

"Sandy's dead. She drowned in the pool," Chase said. "We didn't find Jeb, but someone is in the basement. I'm going down there to check it out. It has to be Jeb, right?" Chase saw Gloria and bent down to check on her. "What happened to her?" he asked.

"Robbie and Gloria were in here together. She choked or something," Jay said. "She's dead too."

"What the hell is going on here?" Katie said, starting to panic. "This is unreal. This cannot be happening." Katie and Melanie began to sob and hug each other.

"We need to get help," Chase said. "Melanie has tried her phone but has no service here. My phone is in the car."

"We don't have service either," Jay replied, "but Robbie left about fifteen minutes ago to get some help. He was going to drive down the road until he could get service and call the police and Gloria's parents."

"And he's not back yet?" Chase asked. "That's pretty fucked up. Jeb is missing too. Something's not right. Their girlfriends are dead, and they're missing."

"What are you gettin' at?" Jay asked in a slightly confrontational tone.

"I'm not trying to get at anything but the truth," Chase replied. "It is what it is. The facts are what they are." Chase and Jay moved toward one another.

"I've been tired of your shit all night," Jay said, getting into Chase's face.

They fought, and the girls yelled for them to stop. Then Melanie watched as Chase grabbed his own head and spun around. Chase said he saw Sandy standing in the corner where she was smiling and watching him. Jay got the upper hand on Chase and punched him a few times in the head.

Suddenly, Chase's eyes grew very big. Melanie could see Sandy's attack on Chase. Sandy's face was right in front of Chase. Her mouth opened wide as if to swallow his head. He freaked out so badly that he fell to the ground and shook uncontrollably.

Melanie heard Jay state that he felt responsible for what had happened to Chase because he had punched him in the jaw, and then Chase's shaking had started. Melanie had watched as Chase had fallen and landed on top of Gloria.

All of a sudden, Gloria's arms wrapped around Chase. She breathed on his neck and told him how much she desired him. She was squeezing him around his chest. He was trying to break free from her grasp. He began breathing heavily. She licked him across the face with her snakelike tongue. Then suddenly, it all stopped.

Gloria was still. The room was still. Chase was still. Melanie stood there in utter fear because of everything that she had witnessed. She could not explain what she had experienced in the pool or in this room. There was no explanation for what she had seen and the things she had felt. It was the unreal made real. It horrified her.

"Chase, are you okay?" Katie said. "Chase!" She and Melanie bent down on the floor next to Chase.

While patting his face, Melanie said, "Chase, wake up. C'mon, Chase, wake up."

Katie watched as Jay bent over Chase and lifted his head and shoulders to move him off Gloria. Katie could tell that Chase was startled at first but then seemed to come to his senses. She observed him take a few deep breaths before trying to speak.

"Gloria's alive," he mumbled.

"What are you saying," Katie replied. "You're not making any sense, Chase."

"She was squeezing me," he continued to mumble.

"Chase! Come on, man. You gotta pull it together," Jay said.

"He's not making any sense, right?" Katie said. "She couldn't have moved."

"I don't know, Katie, but we all need to get up now and get out of here," Melanie said.

"Help me sit him up," Jay said. "We need to wait here until help arrives. It can't be much longer if Robbie got through on his phone. Let's just stay together and calm down."

Katie watched as Jay closed and locked the door to the bedroom. She felt as though they were trying to keep out a burglar. Something about this didn't feel like the common burglar though. Katie was reminded of all of her daydreams, drawings, and the common themes that ran through them. They were dark and disturbing. They contained visions of blood, death, and a tall figure with crimson eyes. Katie could sense the danger that they would face in the hours ahead. She knew they needed to get out of the house right away.

11 FAMILY TIES BEFORE ONE MORE DIES

After entering the basement, Robbie was sure that he would find the source of the laughter he had heard. He searched the three large rooms for the source, but he could not find one. He did find a lot of junk, which had been piled in the basement. It looked as though it had been stored there for a long time. The boxes looked dusty and old. *What is all of this stuff doing down here?* Robbie wondered.

As he browsed through the first room, he found boxes piled on boxes. The boxes contained years of personal items like clothes, toys, towels, blankets, books, jewelry, dishes, silverware, and more. The shelves contained more of the same. He looked in another room and found games, cards, pillows, glasses, holiday decorations, and other household items.

When he entered the third room, he noticed that it contained very little in the way of stored items. It was the smallest of the three rooms. He wondered why two rooms were packed with stuff and one room was almost empty. The room was shaped disproportionately to the house as well. Everything about the basement didn't seem right and didn't make sense—the look, the feel, and the smell.

He found himself being drawn to some of the items in the first room, so he went back in there. He was curious to know a little more about the people who had once lived in the house. Obviously, the oddly shaped room in the basement was not the only thing that made him curious. He had listened to the tales that some of the elders in the town had told. He had heard kids retelling their parents' stories.

The basement was cold—much colder than the rest of the house and even colder than it was outside. Every corner seemed dark, even when the lights were on. The colors on the walls and the trim were varied shades of gray. The concrete floor had been painted. The doors had recently been replaced and painted a bright-white color. The doors and the lights seemed to reflect strange shadows, which rose up from the darkness in the corners.

The place gave Robbie a creepy feeling, but he had witnessed something so bizarre that he had to have answers before he could leave the house. He felt that he would find those answers somewhere in the boxes. He just had to search.

He started in the first room, which was the biggest room and had the most boxes. He opened a few boxes that contained pictures and frames. As he looked through each box, he could tell that the pictures were old. He searched for photos that had names and dates, but there were only a few of them.

He came across a picture of an older woman with a young child named Gregory. He couldn't have been more than five years old. The woman in the picture was in a fancy dress. He could tell that she was a financially secure woman. He looked at other pictures and found several more of Gregory with that same woman and a man whom Robbie assumed was Gregory's father. Their clothes were old. Robbie thought that maybe they were from the 1940s or 1950s.

He looked through another box and found more of the same, except that Gregory and his parents appeared to be getting older. Robbie assumed that any other people he saw were family members and friends. He believed that because he saw pictures of only Gregory with his parents in many family photos, Gregory must have been an only child.

Another little girl seemed to be in many of the photos. She and her parents must have been good friends or relatives of Gregory's family. He wanted to keep searching until he found something about her.

The first picture he had found had shown her parents holding a baby girl. He knew that she must have been the little girl in the other pictures. He would search until he found more.

The fifth box that he opened had many framed photos. The photos were of two teenagers. Right away, he identified the male as Gregory. He couldn't be sure that the girl was the same one that he had found in so many pictures before. She looked like the little girl, but he felt some doubt.

He opened the frame, hoping to find something written on the picture. He got lucky. It said, "Gregory and Lucy, July 1953." Gregory looked older than Lucy did. She appeared to be about fourteen or fifteen years old. He had to be seventeen or eighteen years old. Either way, Robbie thought that they must have grown up together. Based on the number of pictures he saw of them together, he thought that they had the approval of their parents for their relationship.

Robbie continued to open box after box, viewing pictures and getting a real feel for the family that had lived in the house. He was not getting any closer to what had happened to Gloria though.

Robbie continued his search. From what Robbie could tell, Gregory and Lucy had three children. The girls' names were Rebecca, Samantha, and Carolyn. They were born in the late 1950s and early 1960s. One picture of the three girls identified them as the Hamilton sisters. That reference reminded him of the stories that he had heard about the Hamilton women who lived in that house. *Of course, they are only stories*, he thought. There had never been any proof of anything. No one had witnessed anything that could be verified. They had just been the Hamilton family or the Hamilton sisters, who had lived in that house out on Highway 89. His thoughts ran wild.

Robbie had heard stories that the Hamilton family had practiced witchcraft and that the three Hamilton sisters had been witches like their mother and ancestors. Although they were a friendly group of people, they were also very private and kept to themselves. The sisters attended public school. They were said to have been very smart, but they didn't interact much with other children at school. They were friends with only a select group of families in town.

The Garrison family had once owned most of the land in the area around Salem. If you wanted to live peacefully in or around Salem, you had to be at peace with the Garrisons. Robbie found it on the back of a picture of an older woman: Lucille Garrison Hamilton. Lucy was a Garrison. A marriage between family fortune and community prestige had been prearranged for Lucy and Gregory. They were a power couple indeed. The town's witch married the town's mayor. What more was there to discover?

Robbie heard glass breaking in the other room. He

asked, "Who's there?" but heard no reply. Glass broke again and then again. He contemplated whether to hide or confront the thing that was breaking glass.

When he stepped into the other room to confront it, an empty glass jar rolled to his feet. He tried to step around it, but in that moment, the glass jar broke, sending glass into the air. The pieces of the glass jar were suspended in midair for a moment, and then they returned slowly back to their original form and rested at his feet. Then the intact jar rolled away from him in the same direction from which it came. The glass kept repeating the same action over and over. *But why?* he wondered.

Again, he watched it roll into the room and stop at his feet. He let the glass finish its process, only this time he followed the glass back to where it came from. It led him to a box with more pictures and frames. This box contained pictures of Carolyn with her two daughters, Evelyn and Erica. There were a couple of pictures of Carolyn with a man named Charles Davidson, but it appeared that they had never married.

Charles had mysteriously disappeared just after Evelyn (Li'l Evie) was born. The box also contained news articles about his disappearance. There were at least two organized search parties, and they dragged a local lake. Evidently, his disappearance raised questions about the practice of witchcraft in the Hamilton household, but Gregory publicly denied such rumors repeatedly.

There were more articles about unexplained disappearances or deaths in the area, all mentioning connections to the Hamilton family and the possibility of them being victims of witchcraft. *Is that what happened to Gloria? Was she the victim of a Hamilton family witch?* Robbie wondered. *That has to be it. Now I need to let everyone know what we're facing. Help should be here by now.*

He ran for the stairs. As he headed up them, he heard glass breaking all over the basement. He turned the knob of the basement door, but the door would not open. He tried forcing the door open by throwing his shoulder into it, but the door didn't budge. Just as he started yelling for help, the glass stopped breaking. A single glass jar rolled to the bottom step of the stairwell. He contemplated whether he should go down the stairs or just keep yelling for someone to help. He decided to go down to the bottom step. He moved slowly and carefully, looking all around.

The jar rolled toward the smallest room. It stopped when it reached a brick wall. Robbie stepped down and moved toward the jar. He approached it with caution and noticed that the wall it had stopped at was missing some bricks. Peeking through the hole, he could tell that there was another room beyond the brick wall. He removed a couple of bricks to get a better look into the room. It seemed older than the rest of the house. There were jars and books everywhere. The room looked as though it had not been updated. Furniture and belongings in the room were old and worn. He couldn't see what was in the jars.

He grabbed a metal bar, which had been used to hold weights, and used it to break another brick free. When he did this, another jar rolled over and stopped at his feet. He immediately felt a chill in the air, and his heart began to race. He took a step away from the wall in the direction of the stairs. When he did, the glass jar broke. Robbie decided to run for the stairs. Once he had reached the bottom step, he stopped dead in his tracks.

Slowly, he backed up against the wall. Immediately, he felt an intense burning sensation on his skin. Something on the wall was burning through his clothing to his flesh. He tried to move away from the wall, but it tore at his flesh as he moved. He screamed in agony. Suddenly, he lifted his head. He now saw more clearly what had stopped him from running up the stairs. The floor was covered with them: timber rattlesnakes and copperheads everywhere, slithering throughout the rooms. He tried to pretend that they were not there and were just in his imagination, but when he pulled away from the wall and stepped out, two snakes struck immediately at his leg.

Again, he felt his skin being seared by the wall as he moved backward away from the snakes. The snakes were gathering at his feet. One snake was making its way up his body. In fear, he moved his head back to keep the snake away from his face. His head stuck to the wall, and the wall burned it. Again, he screamed from the pain.

He attempted to move away from the wall, but that action pulled the flesh from his back, exposing torn flesh and tissue along the length of his body. The snakes struck, one after another. Somehow, he managed not to fall.

A metal blade from a handsaw flew from across the room, cut into his midsection, and lodged into the wall. Another flew from the back corner of the room and pinned his right leg against the wall, cutting through bone and flesh. Several more, one after the other, flew from across the room and trapped him against the wall, which continued to melt his skin.

The snake climbed up his body to his face. It cocked its head to the side as if it were reading his reactions to pain. The wall was still searing his flesh. Poisonous snakes were biting him. Metal saw blades had cut through his skin and bone to pin him to the wall. Yes, his face was showing pain. The snake saw it, which meant It saw his pain too.

Robbie began to hear voices and saw a shadowy figure approaching him. It was in a long, black robe and carried what appeared to be a hammer with a large metal head. The voice spoke to him in a deep, sinister tone. "Are you afraid?" It said. It leaned forward and breathed on the side of Robbie's face. It flicked Its tongue against Robbie's face. Robbie yelled in pain and fear.

He wondered how much more could he endure. A snake slithered upward and behind Robbie's neck. He was bleeding from the various parts of his body where the metal saw blades pinned him to the wall.

It stepped back from Robbie and looked at him as he bled and suffered. It waved Its hand. When It did, every saw blade began spinning in place, cutting and tearing into Robbie's skin, muscle, and bone. Robbie gurgled from the blood bubbling up his throat. It watched him closely. The blades stopped spinning, and Robbie's body fell forward off the wall, which ripped his burnt flesh off his body. It lifted Robbie's face and stared into his eyes. Robbie saw the shape of a skull on one side of the face under the hood of the robe. Robbie tried to move and break free from Its hold.

"All those dreams of football shattered by your greatest fears: torn muscles, broken bones, and irreparable injuries," It said and then laughed heartily. It swung the metal hammer at Robbie's knees and then his elbows. The sound of cracking bones echoed throughout the room.

"A man of your size having a fear of snakes? Shame on you. You're a disgusting excuse for a man. How could you be afraid of these beautiful, friendly pets?"

It continued laughing as It took a handful of snakes and put them to Robbie's face. They attacked viciously. Snakes covered his body, biting him all over. Robbie just lay there. He was in too much pain to vocalize his screams. Then in a flash, the snakes were gone and so was It.

12 A PLAN LEADS TO DIRECT CONFRONTATION

Being behind a locked door did not make Katie feel any safer. Katie could tell that her friends were growing more and more impatient. She was wondering what had happened to Robbie and the help he was supposed to get for them.

"This is ridiculous. What are we waiting for?" Chase asked. "You heard those screams."

"That sounded like Robbie," Katie said. "Someone should go check on him."

"We aren't really sure what we heard," Jay said. "We're safer if we all stay together."

"Then maybe we should all go check on Robbie," Melanie said.

"No. We're staying right here until help comes," Jay said. "We have to stay together to be safe."

"Gloria wasn't alone when this happened to her," Melanie said.

"You heard those screams," Chase said as he moved in to whisper to Jay. "Men don't scream like that. He's hurt and hurt bad, dude."

"We'll wait five more minutes for help to come," Jay said. "If no one shows up, all of us will go together to search downstairs for Robbie and Jeb."

Katie shook as Chase punched the wall, showing his disagreement with Jay's decision, but she was grateful that he chose not to argue with Jay. She and Melanie also accepted the decision and kept hoping for help to come.

"Hey, look just beyond the pool in the shadows. Do you see it?" Jay said as he looked out the window. "It's a robed man with red eyes lookin' right up at us." The others scrambled to the window to see what Jay saw, but they saw nothing.

"Where?" Chase asked.

"Upper left corner of the pool just inside those bushes," Jay replied.

"I don't see anything," Melanie said.

"I don't either," Chase said.

Jay got angry. "He's right there! How can you not see him?"

"I'm trying, Jay, but I don't see him either," Katie replied.

Jay looked again. He stood there and watched the robed man watching them.

Chase suddenly said, "There he is. He's by the edge of the shed. I see him, Jay."

"No, you don't because he hasn't moved," Jay said. "He's still standing where I told you he was, and he's watching us."

"Well, he can't be because I see a man in a dark robe with red eyes over by the shed," Chase said.

"Where, Chase? Let me see him," Melanie said. She looked out the window but saw nothing. "I don't see either one of those men."

"Let me look," Katie said. "Either you both are lying to scare us or there are two men out there who are trying to kill us."

"There's only one, and I'm not sure it's a man," Jay said. "I'm not sure what it is."

"There must be two if we're both seeing him at the same time in two different places," Chase added.

While they were debating whether one or two robed men were in the backyard, Katie was looking out of the window and trying to see them. Finally, she did, only the man was not where either of them had said he was. He was now at the closest corner of the pool just under the window. She stepped back from the window. She looked alarmed, and Melanie noticed it.

"Katie, what's wrong?" Melanie asked.

"It's him. He's just under the window at the corner of the pool," Katie said in a frantic voice.

Chase raced over to the window to look first. "No, he's not," Chase said. "He hasn't budged from where I said he was standing by the shed."

Jay also looked out the window again. "The one I'm seeing is still there too," Jay said.

"That makes three," Katie said. "Are there three men after us, Jay?"

"No, there has to be an explanation," Jay said. "It must be some sort of projection or something."

"If they're all out there, they're not downstairs or anywhere else in this house," Chase said. "I locked every door and braced the basement door before we came up here."

"We still can't be sure that they don't have some way to access the downstairs," Jay said.

While they discussed the possibilities of going downstairs to the basement to see if Robbie or Jeb was hurt, Katie decided to look out the window again. As she peeked above the edge of the windowsill, she was met head-on by the upper half of the man in the black robe. Stunned, she fell backward and screamed. It passed through the wall to enter the room. The others were unable to see what she saw, but they could tell she was seeing something play out before her eyes. They swung at the air, but nothing stopped her from seeing It.

As It approached her, she saw that Its left leg had a large cloven hoof. One side of Its face was a skull. It had two red eyes that almost burned a hole right through her. She suspected that It was a male due to Its large size, but she had no way of truly knowing that. She knew that It was standing inches from her and glaring at her as if she were Its prey. It glanced downward at her neck and then disappeared.

Katie began to breathe again. She had been holding her breath the whole time It was in her face. She jumped up and told the group to run. Jay grabbed her by the arm to stop her.

"Stop! What happened?" he asked. "What did you see?"

"Nothing. She saw nothing," Chase said.

"That's bullshit, Chase, and you know it," Jay replied, frustrated with Chase's attitude.

"What is that supposed to mean?" Chase replied, knowing exactly what Jay meant.

"You know what I'm talking about, Chase."

"Enlighten me, Jay."

Jay grabbed Chase by the shoulders and pinned him against the wall. "She was seeing something. We have all been seeing things. You too," Jay said. He turned back to Katie. "What did you see, Katie?"

"Something in a black robe with a half-covered face. It had a skull on one side, a leg with a cloven hoof, and two red eyes. That's all I saw. It was right here,"

Katie quickly told them with tears in her eyes. She was terrified by what she had just experienced. Melanie tried to comfort her but was afraid as well.

"Okay, we leave here together," Jay said, trying to calm the group.

"It's about time," Chase said.

"Chase, just shut up and listen please," Jay said. "We all stick together, no matter what, once we leave here. Understand?"

"My car is the last one in line," Chase said. "My keys are on the coffee table in the living room. I can grab them, and we can make a run for it."

"That's not the plan, Chase," Jay said.

"What?" Melanie said. "We need to get out of here."

"You're crazy if you're thinking about anything else, Jay," Chase replied in a contemptuous tone.

"Well, I am thinking about something else, Chase," Jay said. "I'm thinking that the sounds you and Melanie heard in the basement could be Jeb or Robbie, and they might need our help."

"We can't go all the way to the basement, Jay," Melanie said.

"If Jeb or Robbie is possibly down there needing our help, we have to try to get to them, Melanie," Katie said as she fought back her tears. "I wouldn't want to be left behind." Katie could tell that Melanie didn't want to go to the basement, but she nodded in agreement with Jay's plan.

"Melanie?" Chase implored. When he realized he had lost Melanie to Jay's plan, Chase let out a deep sigh and said, "What's the plan?"

"I'm going down first," Jay said.

"Bullshit! I'm going first," Chase said.

"Fine! Chase will go down first, and you girls will go down next. I'll follow up the rear," Jay said.

"And you want us to go through the basement door that's off the kitchen?" Chase asked.

"Yes, the one you braced before you came to us. Keep close and stay alert. No matter what you see, just keep movin'," Jay said.

"Is everybody ready?" Chase asked. Katie wanted to answer no, but she knew she had to do it. She definitely did not want to be left upstairs alone. She just was not sure who or what they were going to find when they entered the basement, and she was already frightened enough.

13 THE SECRETS WITHIN

Katie watched as Chase unlocked and opened the bedroom door. She paused behind him in the doorway as he stepped out into the hallway and looked around. After he waved for them to come out of the room, Katie followed behind him. She was frightened and moved so quickly down the stairwell that she slipped and startled all of them. She signaled with her hands that she was okay. The incident had only been an accident and nothing more.

They continued down the stairs, through the living room, and to the basement door near the kitchen. Katie cringed as Chase removed the chair from in front of the door. Then, within seconds, she could see that Chase thought they were in trouble by the look on his face after he removed the chair. Something had caught his attention and had scared the hell out of him.

"Run, girls! Run!" Chase yelled.

At that same time, Katie turned and saw claws striking Jay's back. Katie had noticed that he had moved slightly when Chase yelled. That had prevented the full force of Its claws from striking him, but Katie felt that Jay must be in severe pain. Katie saw Chase grab Jay and help him to the basement door and down the steps. She closed the door behind them. For what seemed like a long time, they watched the door to make sure that nothing was going to open it.

When it seemed safe, Katie moved some boxes so Jay could sit on one rather than the floor. Katie and Melanie started looking for something to put on Jay's cuts. Katie caught herself watching as Jay removed his shirt, revealing toned muscles, which should have had him playing on the football team along with his friends.

Within minutes, Melanie screamed, "No, no, no, no, no. Please, no." She had found Robbie lying on the floor of the basement with multiple deep and wide cuts, burned skin on his back and head, and swelling over a large area of his body. She backed away from him and felt Chase's hands on her shoulders. She pointed, and he saw Robbie.

After looking at him from a distance, he believed that Robbie was dead, but Melanie nudged him to take a closer look. She watched as Chase removed his own letterman jacket to cover Robbie's upper body. When he did, Melanie and Chase heard Robbie let out a whimper.

"Robbie! Dude, just hang in there, man. We're here. We're gonna help ya," Chase said.

"Yeah," Robbie said. His response was weak and labored.

He was lying face down on his stomach with his head turned to the right, which made it even more difficult to hear and understand him. Melanie suggested that they turn him over so that they could hear him better, but Robbie let out a deep groan to express his pain.

"All right, my man. I'm not gonna move you. Let me just put this under the edge of your head," Chase whispered to Robbie, his kind words lacking hope. He lifted Robbie's head and placed his folded jacket sleeve underneath it.

"I'll be right back," Chase said. "Melanie, stay with him."

Melanie could sense the urgency in Chase's voice.

"I have to find something to put on these wounds and stop the bleeding," he said.

"Okay, but please hurry back," she said. "Wait! Is he going to be okay?"

"I, uh, I can't say," he responded. "I will hurry."

Melanie knew there was truth in Chase's words, no matter what happened to Robbie. Chase had chosen a response that made him honest without having to answer her question with a yes or a no. She thought that he really couldn't get himself to say no, even if he believed it, because as teammates, he and Robbie had learned the fight wasn't over until it was over. That must be the only way that Chase could look at this situation.

Chase walked to her, stared deeply into her eyes, and kissed her. "We're gonna be okay. I promise," he said.

"You can't break a promise," she replied.

"No, I can't break a promise," he responded.

Katie was trying to clean Jay's cuts with some rags and water from a basement sink when Chase walked back into the room. Jay was seated on top of a couple of sealed boxes, flinching each time she touched him.

"Where did you get that water? I'm going to need some of that too, and some rags," Chase told her.

"There's a sink around the other side of the stairs, and I found these rags in a drawer near the sink," Katie replied. "Did something happen to Melanie?"

"No, it's not Melanie," Chase replied.

That caught Katie and Jay's attention. Both of them looked at him questioningly, but when they did not get a quick enough response from him, they asked almost simultaneously, "Then who is it?"

Chase stopped and looked at them. He looked down and then lifted his eyes to them and said, "It's Robbie."

"Oh my God! Is he okay?" Katie asked. She started to walk in the direction of the third room, but Chase stepped in front of her.

"What are you doing?" Katie asked. She was annoyed by Chase and impatient to check on Robbie. "Get out of the way, Chase!"

"Katie, wait," Chase said. "He's hurt really bad." Katie continued to walk toward the third room anyway.

"How bad?" Jay said. He heard Katie scream.

"I tried to tell her," Chase said.

Jay rushed to Katie's side. She glanced down at Robbie and knew that Robbie's injuries required immediate emergency care. Katie sat down on the floor beside Robbie and looked for a place to touch him so that she could show how much she cared, but she did not see a place to do so without causing him pain. Her eyes filled with tears, but she tried not to let Robbie hear her cry. The guy she had loved secretly for three years now lay in front of her, enduring unfathomable pain.

Jay sat down on the floor beside Katie to comfort her, and she immediately buried her face in his chest. Soon she spoke to Robbie. "Robbie, it's Katie. I'm here. We're all here." She talked to him as Melanie and Chase tried to clean the cuts on his legs with rags. The cuts were too deep and continued to bleed.

"Robbie, I need to be able to stop the bleeding from these cuts," Chase said. "It will hurt when I tie these rags around your legs, okay?"

A barely audible, "Yeah," came from his mouth.

Katie flinched as Chase pulled tightly on the first rag. Melanie crossed over to comfort Katie, while Jay assisted Chase by tying some rags around the deep cuts in Robbie's legs. The rags appeared to help with those wounds, but there were so many other cuts, Katie feared there was no way to help him.

Robbie attempted to enunciate the word *roll*. He had to say it a few times before Katie really knew what he was saying. He wanted them to roll him onto his back. *Does he really want that?* Katie wondered.

"Man, your back is hurt really bad. I don't think that's a good idea," Jay said. He seemed to be reading Katie's mind.

Robbie became more adamant. He more forcefully and clearly said, "Roll."

There just did not appear to be a good place to grab hold of him so that they could turn him over. They started by looking for places that were not cut or burned. They carefully moved their hands underneath him to get him onto his side first and then lowered him onto his back. He yelled in pain multiple times during the process.

Katie watched as Jay cringed but pushed onward with the task at hand. From the look on Chase's face, Katie knew that he must have considered it the hardest play ever executed on the field. Katie saw Melanie turn away so that she would not have to watch them move Robbie. Katie heard Robbie cry out continuously as they rolled him over. Soon and as quickly as they could, the painful deed was done. He was lying on his back.

Now that he was in this position, Katie could better view his injuries. She knew they were serious, and after rolling him over, they only seemed worse. His face and neck were swollen. He had deep cuts that were still bleeding. Chase and Jay continued to tie rags over the wounds to help control the bleeding, but it didn't appear to help much. Katie was startled as Robbie grabbed Melanie's wrist and tried to talk to her. She and Melanie leaned in closely. Melanie put her ear next to his mouth.

"I think he is trying to say 'box,'" Melanie told the group.

"Wait, let me listen." Katie put her ear next to his mouth, and he repeated the same sound. "I think she's right," she said. "I think he is saying 'box.'"

"But what box?" Jay said, frustrated. "There are dozens of them in here."

"Robbie, what box?" Melanie asked him. He mumbled a response but it was not audible.

"Damn it!" Chase said. He kicked one of the boxes. "We can't catch a fuckin' break here."

Katie leaned in near Robbie's mouth to listen more intently. Robbie continued to make inaudible responses.

"It's okay, Katie," Jay said. "You tried."

"And I'm still trying," Katie snapped.

Jay knew to back off. He knew Katie had her mind made up. She was going to figure out what Robbie was trying to say, so there was no point in trying to get her to give up.

"Everyone, without looking all at once, please tell me if you can see a tall figure standing in the corner near the far window," Chase said.

Since Melanie had her back toward the window, she was not able to respond to Chase's question right away. Jay's response was no and so was Katie's.

"Well, I've figured out what Robbie has been trying to say," Melanie said.

"What is it?" Jay asked.

"He's been saying, 'Behind you,'" Melanie responded. At the moment she spoke those words, she was grabbed from behind and dragged backward until her body stopped flat and hard against the concrete wall. She was lifted by the neck and off her feet with force. Then she dropped to the floor, choking and bruised.

"Where is it, Chase?" Melanie asked.

"I-I-I don't know," Chase stuttered and then yelled in fear. Katie had been holding onto Robbie's hand. She now moved quickly into the corner of the small room near the place where Robbie had been removing bricks from the wall earlier that night. Jay went to Katie's side and sat down beside her.

"Chase, I'm really scared. Where is it?" Melanie asked him once again.

"I don't know, Melanie," he yelled back. "I don't see it."

"Shh, do you hear that?" Katie asked.

"That's Robbie. He's trying to speak again," Jay

said. He moved over next to Robbie to put his ear near Robbie's mouth. Jay was able to understand what Robbie said but didn't know what it meant. "He said the word 'bricks,' but what does he mean?"

"He's said 'box' and 'bricks,'" Katie said.

"Look in the boxes," Jay said. "He must have been going through them looking for something."

"Yeah, stuff has been taken out of many of the boxes," Katie said.

"It looks to me like Robbie was browsing through some pictures in these boxes over here," Melanie said.

"Same here," Katie said.

"There are pictures and articles in these boxes," Chase said.

"Just more of the same here," Jay said. "Let me take a look at those articles."

Chase passed the articles to Jay for him to read.

"Robbie, blink your eyes once for yes or twice for no," Chase said. "Is there something in these pictures we need to know?"

Robbie blinked.

"That was once," Melanie said to the group.

"That was definitely a yes," Katie affirmed.

"Were you trying to tell us something about bricks earlier?" Chase asked.

"That was a yes," Melanie said.

"Are the bricks related to what is in the boxes?" Chase asked.

"Again, that was yes," Melanie said.

"All right, we need to learn as much as we can about what's in these boxes as fast as we can," Jay said.

"Thanks, man," Chase told Robbie.

They rushed to look through the stuff that had been removed from the boxes and shared what they had found.

"All of these boxes have pictures of a little boy named Gregory and his parents," Melanie said, "from the time he was a baby until he was a teenager."

"These boxes have pictures of our former mayor, Gregory Hamilton, and his family," Jay said, "especially his daughters, the infamous Hamilton sisters: Rebecca, Samantha, and Carolyn."

"Jay and his stories of witches and witchcraft," Melanie said.

"Have you been able to explain anything we have seen or heard here tonight, Melanie?" Katie asked, perturbed.

"Enough. We don't have time for this," Chase said. "Robbie? Do these articles ha—" He stopped in the middle of his sentence. Robbie stared blankly back at him. There was no need to finish his question. It had claimed another life.

"No," Katie said as she sobbed and kneeled down at Robbie's side. Now he would never know how much she cared for him. She held Robbie's hand in hers and squeezed it, hoping he would squeeze back. Melanie sat down beside Katie.

Katie knew that she could lean on her best friend, who knew how much he meant to her. They cried together, and Chase and Jay knew better than to interrupt the moment they were sharing. Katie leaned over and closed Robbie's eyes, and then Chase covered his face with a towel he had found in a box.

Chase said, "We need to—"

"Okay, Chase!" Katie interrupted and went back to the boxes she had been searching through before Robbie had died. Melanie resumed going through her boxes too.

"These boxes have pictures of the Hamilton sisters at various ages in their lives," Katie said. "This is odd," she added.

"What's that?" Jay said.

"I've seen this picture before," she said.

"Which picture?" he said.

"This one of Rebecca," she replied.

"Where have you seen it?" he asked.

"At my grandmother's house," she answered.

"Why would your grandmother have a picture of Rebecca Hamilton?" he inquired.

"I'm not sure, but her first name *is* Rebecca," Katie responded.

"Is your grandmother one of the three infamous Hamilton sisters?" Chase asked.

"The one Hamilton sister who wasn't present in the house on the night the family was killed?" Jay said. "Look at this article." Jay showed them an article about the deaths of the family members. The article stated that Rebecca Hamilton Tipton was married and no longer lived in the family's home. She was not considered a suspect in the murders.

"That's my grandmother's name," Katie said. "That's impossible. She's not a witch." She kept looking for more pictures and articles for some explanation. The more she looked through the boxes, the more things she found that seemed to be familiar to her.

"This article identifies the family members who died in this house: Gregory Hamilton, Lucy Garrison Hamilton, Jeffrey Marks, Samantha Hamilton Marks, Carolyn Hamilton, and her daughter Erica," Chase said. "Carolyn's other daughter, Evelyn, died at the hospital."

"I'm confused," Melanie said. "Are we actually saying we believe that dead witches who are somehow related to Katie are responsible for killing our friends tonight?"

"This doesn't make any sense," Katie said. "Why would my own family want to harm me?"

"And if they are the ones trying to kill us," Jay said, "who killed them?"

"Nothing is making sense," Katie said. "There has to be something we're still missing."

"The bricks!" Melanie said. "We still don't know what Robbie meant by the bricks."

"Check the walls," Chase said.

"Nothing over here," Jay said as he checked an interior brick wall.

"Oh no! No, not Jeb!" Katie said as she looked out a window with a view of the shed. She was able to tell the gruesome way in which Jeb had been killed. The others came running to look out the window and comfort her.

"Sandy, Gloria, Jeb, Robbie. It's killing all of us," Melanie yelled at It. "Come and get me! What are you waiting for?"

"Melanie, stop. Don't challenge It or invite It here," Jay said.

"I don't care anymore," she responded as if she had some newly found courage. "It's going to kill us all anyway."

"Stop it, Melanie," Jay said.

The moment that he told her to stop, It appeared in a dark robe with Its cloven foot and struck her across the back with Its claws. She fell to the floor, and It disappeared as quickly as It had appeared. Katie grabbed wet rags to wipe down Melanie's cuts. They weren't deep, so she was very lucky. It was as if It had been playing with her.

Suddenly, Chase was pushed straight into the back wall by an unseen force. They knew It must be after him. They tried to help him by grabbing hold of his hands, but he told them It was gone. Again, It was playing with them.

Jay continued to search all the brick walls and came to the one in the small room. He told the others that some of the bricks had been removed from that wall. He looked through the hole and told them that he saw another room. The others gathered around as Jay kept removing loose bricks. The opening was large enough for them to climb through.

"This has to be what Jay meant by bricks," Jay said.

"Definitely," Katie said.

"Did anyone find a flashlight in any of the boxes?" Jay asked.

"Wait," Chase said. "I recall finding some candles in a box over here."

"Great! What about some matches or a lighter?" Jay said.

"Check Robbie's pocket for a lighter," Chase said. "He had thought about making a small bonfire out here tonight."

Jay checked Robbie's pockets and found a lighter. Jay said that he was going in the room first. The girls were to follow him, and Chase was to come last. Jay climbed through the hole in the wall. They passed him a couple of lit candles. He said everything was okay, so he helped the girls through the hole and gave the lit candles to them.

Finally, Chase came through the hole. Just as he

did, It appeared right at the entrance and was in Chase's face. It waved Its arm and knocked Chase against a wall and cornered him there. He was stuck, and he could not move.

Katie yelled at It. "Stop! Just stop! You're a coward! Leave us alone." Chase's body was dropped to the floor, as if Katie's words carried some power with them.

"We're running out of time," Jay said. "That thing is going to get tired of playing with us."

"I agree," Chase said. "We need to make a run for my car and get out of here."

"We have no one left to find or save but ourselves," Melanie said. "I agree with Chase. We need to get out of here."

"No, the answers to all of this could be right here in this room," Katie said. "I can't just leave now."

"I will stay with Katie," Jay said. "If you two want to make a run for it, you can go. Send back some help."

"We will," Chase said. "Melanie, let's go."

Chase and Melanie climbed back through the hole, leaving Katie and Jay to search the contents of this secluded room. Now they were separated in their efforts to survive the night.

THE CHASE ENDS

Chase and Melanie made their way back through the room and past Robbie's body. Melanie's tears began almost instantly. The two paused for just a moment, as Melanie sought reassurance that separating was the right thing to do.

"Are we sure that we should leave instead of staying to help them fight this thing?" Melanie asked frantically.

"Think about what you just said," Chase said. "We don't even know what this thing is, never mind how to fight it. Why are we even debating this?"

"Shouldn't we stay and at least watch their backs while they search through the contents of that room?" Melanie asked. "The answer may be in there."

"Melanie, if you want to stay, stay, but I'm getting the hell outta here," Chase said. "I will send help as soon as I can." He started to leave.

133

"Wait!" Melanie said. Melanie looked at him, looked back at the doorway leading to the hidden room, and then looked at Chase once again before deciding to leave with him. The lights flickered, reminding them that either option they chose would be dangerous.

They ran toward the stairs, past boxes, which were on both sides of them. When they looked at the top of the stairs, it seemed to be a mile away. The door creaked open about four inches. It was almost as if something approved of their decision, which created great unrest for Melanie.

What did they have to do? They had to make it up the basement stairs, grab Chase's keys, pass through the front breezeway and open stairwell, go out the front door, and pass through the front yard to get to Chase's car, which was along the side of the house. This escape route seemed like the shortest distance to the car. As Chase drove, Melanie would call 911 until she could get through to someone. Now all they needed to do was execute their plan, which was going to be much harder than creating it.

They took each step one at a time while watching all around them. Chase was standing directly in front of Melanie as he pushed open the door. Then, that all changed.

"Chase?" She called to him, as she suddenly found herself at the foot of the stairs.

Chase turned around and went down a few steps. "What are you doing? C'mon."

She had climbed the stairs with Chase. She was confused by what had happened. She walked up the steps again to Chase, but getting close to him seemed very difficult to do. With every step she took, she seemed to take a step backward. She just wasn't able to climb the stairs.

"C'mon, Melanie, quit messin' around," Chase said. Chase was watching for It to reveal Itself on the other side of the door. She ran up the stairs and found that she was getting closer to him, but the steps seemed to go on forever. Finally, she reached him and took his hand.

"What is wrong with you? Why are you breathing so hard?" Chase asked. "Are you okay?"

"Did you not see that I've been running?" she responded. "Didn't you just watch me run up those stairs multiple times?"

"No, you have been standing there staring up at me like you were changing your mind again," Chase said. "I've been watching for the right moment to make our next move."

Then she watched as his eyes grew big. He dropped her hand. Chase saw It appear at the bottom of the stairwell. He turned toward the door and ran, leaving Melanie stuck on what became a never-ending escalator. No matter how hard she tried, she could not reach the doorway. Now Chase had left her all alone.

It appeared to Chase again, with Its cloven foot and long, black robe. It stopped Chase dead in his tracks. Its long, slender, bone-like claws reached out and touched Chase's brow. It disappeared, but Chase still could not move.

Out of nowhere, It suddenly reappeared and used Its claw to open up Chase's abdomen. Chase watched as his stomach and intestines poured out. He was holding his intestines in his hands and trying to put them back inside. Then It came up behind him and slashed him across the back with Its claws, exposing bone and tissue.

It spoke to him in his football coach's voice. "You're not much of a mover and a shaker right now, are you boy?" the coach said before laughing at him. "You disappoint me. Stick those guts back in there and get to runnin' this field. I said go, boy."

Suddenly, he was no longer holding his guts or feeling any claw marks across his back. He started to run toward the door, but he was swooped up as if he were in a tornado. As he was twisting and swirling around, he kept seeing the face of the thing that had been killing them. It taunted him.

Chase thought about how It could kill him, but It chose not to do so. Why was It just playing with him? What did It want? Did It just enjoy watching people suffer before It killed them, or was It just feeding on their fear? Chase realized that was it. It loved to watch them because they were so afraid of It. The more fear they showed, the more It played with them.

"I'm not afraid of you anymore," Chase said. "Do you hear me? I'm not afraid."

A loud, rough, deep voice, which he had not heard before, said, "You are not afraid anymore, huh?" It laughed at him. It appeared and stopped the tornado that Chase had been stuck inside. It grabbed Chase's face and squeezed his cheeks together. It held him up high and then stomped Its foot. The floor fell out from beneath them. It put Chase on a flimsy hook, which was on the wall and could break at any moment. "Now talk to me about fear," It said.

Chase yelled for help. A fiery pit of molten lava was beneath Chase. It was spinning as if it had a large tornado within it. The sounds of men and women screaming and crying in pain could be heard from the pit. Creatures from within the pit would attempt to reach Chase's legs and try to pull on him, hoping to break the hook from which he dangled.

One creature with webbed hands and a snakelike tongue grabbed Chase's leg. One side of the creature's face had been ripped open. Chase could see the creature's veins, bones, and muscles. It had no nose and only holes in the sides of its head for ears. One eye socket remained intact while the other was fully exposed. The creature had a short body compared to its long legs. It held onto one of Chase's legs while it pulled itself upward, grabbing Chase around the thigh with its mouth, sinking its sharp teeth into him.

Chase's screams echoed throughout the house yet fell on deaf ears. After his screams became louder, the fiery pit suddenly disappeared. He remained suspended in midair and with no floor underneath him. Now he was about two hundred feet above the top of the house. As he realized the distance between him and the ground below, he began to tremble with fear.

Chase had struggled with a fear of heights since he was seven years old. At that time, he almost fell from a bridge while on an outing with his older brother. They were riding bikes when his brother dared him to get close to the edge of the bridge and walk along it. While he was doing so, a passing train caused him to stumble just enough that he found himself hanging on to the side of the bridge. His brother was able to pull him to safety, but the fear of falling always remained.

It knew his fear. It appeared before him and began to beat him with Its mighty fists. It ripped his flesh with Its mighty claws. It dangled him upside down, just to watch him scream and cry like a child who had a toy taken from him.

Chase begged It to let him go, so It did. It dropped him and then grabbed his back, breaking it. It dropped him again and then caught him by the leg, breaking it. It dropped him again and then caught him by the arm, breaking it. The sound of the snapping and cracking of bones could be heard each time he was caught. Each time It dropped and caught him, It brought him closer and closer to the ground.

Finally, It dropped and caught him by the head. It twisted his head before letting him hit the floor of the living room. His body was shaped like a ragdoll as it lay there. The breaking of his neck ended the torture that he had faced at the hand of It that had no name.

MELANIE RACES FOR HER LIFE

It was as if she had been in a vacuum where sound only echoed within the stairwell, which had been endless. She had heard Chase's cries for help but had been unable to get to him.

Now the stairs were back to normal. She no longer had to run endlessly. Melanie felt exhausted. She sat for a second to rest and then quickly pulled herself together as she realized that Chase needed her. She ran to the living room.

Melanie found Chase lying on the living room floor. Obviously, his neck had been twisted and broken. His body had been broken in so many places, it was difficult to see where his joints were. She looked at him, with his perfect brown hair and crystal-blue eyes. A drop of blood rolled from his mouth down his cheek. She wiped it away with her sleeve.

He is even beautiful now, she thought. She lay down on the floor beside him and cuddled him as if he was going to wake up at any moment. It was as if she couldn't accept what she was seeing and was waiting for something to change. But nothing was going to change.

Melanie's stoic look meant that she believed everything was going to be okay. She showed no more emotions. She shed no more tears. She felt at peace lying next to Chase, and that was all that mattered to her. Her dark-brown hair lay loosely on him as she lay next to him. Her arm rested comfortably around his waist. She looked out into the room but really did not see anything in it.

She must have lay there for more than fifteen minutes before the things that were changing around her caught her attention. The room was changing slowly to reflect the living room of her own home. She blinked a few times and looked around the room. She had almost forgotten the danger that was all around her. She sat up and realized that she was in her own living room at home, but she wasn't and knew that—sort of. A hand came from up out of the floor and grabbed her ankle and then another hand. She started pulling against them and fighting back.

Suddenly, her father appeared in the room and spoke to her. "Run to your car, sweetie," he said. "Run."

Her father had made her swear that she would not damage her car in any way when he had bought it for her. Now he was telling her to use it as an escape. He understood her situation. Her greatest fear was that she would damage that car and suffer the wrath of her father, who was capable of inflicting severe emotional pain and suffering. Her car was her only way out. She just had to get her keys from the kitchen counter and make it out one of the doors.

She pulled away from the hands that had grabbed her. She got up and ran toward the kitchen. It appeared in the doorway. She had almost run right into It. She turned to go the other way, and It appeared in front of her again. She felt boxed in. When she turned again and It reappeared, she attempted to run past It. When she did, It caught her and scratched Its claws across her arm. She screamed in fear but still managed to grab her car keys and get out the sliding glass doors that led to the pool.

She passed the pool and the tool shed. Near the tool shed, she slipped on something. She had forgotten who was lying there. A hand grabbed her ankle, and she heard a voice begging for help.

"No, there's no way," she said. "I saw you. You're dead." The source of the voice continued to hold onto her leg and call out for help. Had he really been dead when she saw him? "It's not possible," Melanie continued. "Jeb, you can't be helped. Let go of me."

Another hand grabbed her by the leg. When she reached out to pull Jeb upward, she watched as Jeb's body separated down the middle where it had been ripped into two sections by the meat hook. Melanie had had enough. She freaked out. She started stomping on Jeb's hands and his body's remains. "You're dead, Jeb," Melanie emphasized each word she spoke. "Stay dead, Jeb. Leave me alone. Just leave me alone!" she screamed as she ran away from Jeb's body and toward her car.

In an instant, something came up beside her and pinned her against her car. It had the face of a dog with rows of teeth as sharp as a shark. It had a body as muscular as that of a werewolf. It had claws as sharp as one. Its hair was thin, and its skin was more like that of a man's. It sniffed her all over and held her against the car. She pushed and beat on the animal, but it just growled and gnashed its teeth.

It was there, watching the beast attack her. She saw It out of the corner of her eye. It was next to her. Now It was farther away. Now It was over there. Finally, Melanie challenged It. "If you want me, come get me yourself," Melanie said. "Come on. Come get me!"

The animal pulled back away from her. It sunk backward into the shadows. She jumped into her car. She had to back out around Chase's car, which was parked behind her. Once she did, she expected It to challenge her in some way. She thought It would come after her. Maybe she had shown It enough bravery to get away from It. Now she would get help for Katie and Jay.

She took off down Highway 89 toward town. She only had to drive about four miles before she would have cellular service. Then she remembered that her phone was back at the house. That meant she would have to go to the closest neighbor and use that person's phone.

As she drove, she heard her father's voice again. "Don't wreck that car or else," he told her.

"I'm not, Daddy, I promise," she said.

"You're speeding, Melanie," her father said to her. "Look how fast you're going."

"My friends are in trouble, Daddy," Melanie responded. She looked at her speedometer, which was continuing to climb from 80 to 120 miles per hour. She tried pressing on the brake to slow down, but that did not work.

She was just about to reach the nearest neighbor's house where she could get help when her car left the road and went straight into a utility pole. It bent the front end of her car like crumpled wrapping paper. Without a seat belt on, Melanie flew out of the driver's seat and halfway through the front windshield. Melanie did not move. There was no sign of life.

People who lived nearby heard the accident and called the police. The man and woman went outside to see if they could help. They called out to Melanie, but they did not move her. The man touched her neck and said that he felt a faint pulse. She was still alive.

The police arrived and started to help. Melanie rambled senselessly about a creature, her friends, and a need for help. No one took anything that she said seriously, until Barnes arrived on the scene. He heard her talking about friends, trouble, a creature, and the house on Highway 89. He also remembered what had happened almost thirty years ago. He immediately made a call to Baker, who had since retired but still did some investigative work for the department on occasion.

At first, Baker disregarded what Barnes said. When Barnes told him that the victim had mentioned a creature, it had caught his attention. Baker thought that they finally might be able to explain what had happened to the Hamilton family years earlier. The detective agreed to meet the ambulance at the hospital.

However, when Barnes returned to the scene, he found that there was no need for an ambulance. Melanie had died while he had been talking on the phone. He walked over to Melanie to feel for a pulse. It was true. There was no pulse. She was dead.

As he started to turn away from her, she rose up and reached out her arms to grab him by the neck. She had a tight grip on his throat. He couldn't breathe. He couldn't understand why no one would stop to help him. He fought with her to get free from her grip. The more he fought, the tighter she gripped him. He was losing consciousness. Everything before his eyes was starting to blur. He fell to his knees and passed out.

When he started to regain consciousness, he heard voices saying that he was going to be alright. He heard one man joking about him getting too old to see a bloody, dead body. *She wasn't dead,* he thought. She had just attacked him. How could she be dead if she had just tried to choke him? He wasn't sure how it had happened but he knew that it definitely had.

He watched as they put her body into a body bag and placed her in an ambulance for transport to the hospital morgue. He would follow the ambulance so he could meet with Baker. He wanted answers and knew he was going to have to go to that house to find them. He hoped that Baker would still be as anxious as he had been thirty years earlier, about finding answers to what happened in that house.

As he followed the ambulance, he could see what was going on inside through the back doors. He thought he saw movement in the body bag. Suddenly, Melanie sat straight up on the gurney. She reached out just like she had when she had been trying to choke him. She twisted her hands as if to wring his neck. Her face and arms looked pale blue.

He blinked his eyes, and she was kneeling on the hood of his car. In that moment, he swerved and almost struck another vehicle. In the next moment, she was gone. She was not on his car, and there was no activity in the back of the ambulance either.

When he arrived at the hospital, Barnes had to break the bad news about the victim being deceased to Baker. He did not know how to explain the other things he had experienced, so he was not sure if he would tell him. He believed Baker would think he was crazy. Baker would accuse him of listening to too many stories and town folklore. He decided Baker needed to know even if he might not believe it.

"You told me the victim was alive, Barnes," Baker said.

"When I was on the phone with you, she was alive," Barnes responded convincingly. "She passed while we were on the phone. Things were crazy at the scene, Baker."

"How so?"

"While I was at the scene, I found the victim lying halfway through the windshield of the car, and I swear she was not dead," Barnes said.

"What do you mean?" Baker asked.

"I mean she tried to kill me," Barnes said

"Oh, Barnes, I don't have time for any of this," Baker said.

"Baker, of all people, I thought you would believe me after what you have seen."

"Some girl has a car crash on Highway 89, mentions a creature, and says her friends need help, and you get me out here to do an interview, but now she's dead. That means no interview. Now you want me to believe that after she was pronounced dead, she tried to kill you. Come on, Barnes, this is a little farfetched," Baker said.

"I was standing in front of the body, and she reached up and tried to choke me. Eventually, I guess I passed out. I was picking myself up off the ground. I think it was a sign to tell me not to ask any questions or to get involved, but we have to get involved. We have a thirty-year-old case we may be able to solve," Barnes said with sincere determination.

"Okay, I tell you what. Count me in," Baker said. "Let's go inspect the body first. I do have a desire to find some answers."

"I think I should head on out to the house just in case there are people who need help," Officer Barnes said. "I will call you after I get there and have a chance to check out the scene."

16
THE BOOK IS DISCOVERED

Everything was so dusty. It had been a very long time since anything in the room had been moved. At first, it appeared that the room only contained more empty jars and glassware, but then they realized that some of the jars contained items they could not identify.

With limited light, they worked their way through the items that lay on a long table. They looked at the jars and tried to determine their contents, but the items were so dark that it was too difficult. At one point, Jay swore that he saw an eyeball in a jar, but Katie didn't see it. He tried to open the jar to prove it, but it wouldn't open. According to Katie, it was a good thing because she really didn't want to see it.

"I don't think we're going to find any answers in these jars," Katie said. "It's hard to search in here with no light."

"I think I can help with that," Jay said as he lit two lanterns that he had found on a small corner table in the back of the room. "That should help some."

They looked around and found news articles everywhere. Some were hanging on the walls, and others were lying on the table and chairs.

Katie and Jay began reading some of the articles to see if they could offer any help in their situation. The topics included mysterious deaths, unexplained disappearances, and commonplace missing persons. In many of the articles, there were direct or indirect connections to the Hamilton family or the Hamilton sisters, such as unexplained deaths of the family's friends, missing family friends, and missing boyfriends of the Hamilton sisters. Most importantly, an article of the unexplained disappearance of Charles Davidson, Carolyn Hamilton's fiancé and father of her children, was there. The list went on. No wonder there were so many stories that had been told by the locals who had grown up in Salem.

"Just like I said, they were witches. This explains a lot. Look at all of this," Jay said.

"We don't know anything for sure," Katie said. "Remember, Rebecca Hamilton is my grandmother. You're talking about my ancestors."

"And they were witches," Jay said. "We're probably standing in the room where they practiced their witchcraft."

"Jay, enough! I need you to stay focused, please," Katie said with an intense expression. "We still have to find something that helps with that thing. None of this explains that."

"No, but this might," Jay said. He had run his hand across a book near some of the missing bricks in the wall.

He picked up a large, heavy book and handed it to her. It was bound in pigskin and contained pages of thick, yellowing parchment paper. The book was old and worn, but the cover had protected it well. The cover was trimmed in gold, and it displayed gold markings and symbols.

Even though they did not understand the meanings of the markings and symbols, they believed the book was very important and just might hold the answers to some of their questions. They sat down, pulled the lantern close to them, and began to read from the book. Immediately, they felt the room grow colder. They could see their breath. Continuing to read was their only option now.

The book began with the history of the Pemberton family in 1804, who lived in the town of Old Salem. It progressed from generation to generation of the family tree. It went from the Pembertons, to the Easleys, to the Garrisons, and to the Hamiltons. It emphasized every third generation, which was when a member of the family would give birth to a trio of daughters who could wield the power of the entire coven when they practiced together.

"I told you they were witches," Jay said.

"Shut up!" Katie said. "But remember, the article said that my grandmother, Rebecca, wasn't in the house the night the family died. The power of the third witch wasn't present to protect them from whatever they faced that night."

She looked at Jay with fear in her eyes. "What could they possibly have faced that would have destroyed a family of practicing witches?" she asked him rhetorically. "Could it be the same thing we're facing now?"

"Keep reading," Jay said anxiously.

The next several pages had symbols and their meanings. Some of the symbols represented earth, air, fire, water, spirit, the four seasons, and the cardinal directions.

"There is so much information here," she said.

"Skip that," Jay said. "What else is in there?"

"The next section of the book contains rituals, religious practices, and spells," Katie said. She was puzzled by how this information would be any help to them.

"Now we're talking," he said.

"What do you mean? I don't see how this information is going to help us. We aren't witches. We don't even know what to do with this book or the information in it." She closed the book and pushed it away in frustration.

She walked away from it, feeling hopeless. She closed her eyes and bowed her head.

Jay opened the book and continued to flip through the pages. "Hey, look! In the back pages of this book, there are descriptions of different warlocks and demons. Maybe your family was attacked by one of them. That could be what is happening to us now."

Katie walked over to look through the book again. When she did, Jay was pulled backward forcibly until he reached the back wall. He slammed hard against it before falling to the floor. Hands came up from the floor all around him and held him down. Katie ran to help him, but he told her to keep reading from the book. She turned so that she could watch him while she read.

"I'm not finding anything in here that we can use," Katie said, feeling helpless. "I don't know what else to do." She ran to him and started pulling him up from the floor. "We have to take a chance, make a run for the car, and try to reach help. We can't stay here any longer."

The hands disappeared. As she helped Jay get to his feet, the house seemed to shift on its foundation, as if there was an earthquake, but Salem didn't have earthquakes. Bricks collapsed and the ceiling caved in at the entryway to the secret room. They were trapped. Escaping from the house was no longer an option. They would have to count on help coming from the outside.

17 POETIC DISCOVERIES

Barnes pulled up outside of the infamous house on Highway 89. It looked like the lights were on throughout the house. He barely saw the cars parked alongside the house because they had been parked there to hide them.

It began to rain as he exited his vehicle. First, he approached the front door and knocked on it. He received no response. Barnes knew that he was in for another unforgettable night in connection with the house at 2148 on Highway 89 in Salem. Since no one answered the door, he tried to open it. The knob turned, and he opened the door. He called out to see if anyone was there, but no one responded. He went inside and began to look around.

He walked through the kitchen and noticed that

liquor bottles were strewn throughout the room. He saw many empty bottles, which caused him to question the blood-alcohol content of the young people who had attended the party. Seeing what he was seeing, he had to consider Melanie's blood-alcohol level as a potential factor in her accident.

So far, he hadn't found anyone in trouble. In fact, he had found no one at all. Now, he wondered if they were hiding from him. He called out to them again. "Okay, kids, come on out! Games are over. Let's go. It's time to go home," he yelled. Still, he heard no reply, and no one came out. He looked behind curtains and under tables. He walked down to the laundry room and checked there.

As he started to go upstairs, the lights flickered. Barnes stopped. He suddenly remembered that he hated the house. He was afraid of the place, and he had come alone. He reached for his radio to call for backup, but he only heard static. He could not get service on his cell phone. He had no way to communicate with the outside.

Because no one had responded to him and he couldn't determine that anyone was in immediate danger, he decided that he would drive back to town and wait for Baker. Then they would come back to the house together. He walked to the door and turned the knob. It came off in his hand, and he could not open the door. The lights flickered again.

He walked to the living room, where he found Chase's broken and lifeless body. He felt for a pulse, even though he knew he would not find one. He wondered what or who could have possibly done this.

He tried the sliding glass doors, but he couldn't open them. He tried to open a window. He could not open any of the windows. Out of fear, he became desperate and tried to break the glass on the windows, but he couldn't do it. He was trapped inside the house that had caused him many nightmares and sleepless nights.

He heard noises: the meow of a cat, the laugh of a clown, and the growl of a dog. He saw things flash before him: a black cat, a clown face, and a rottweiler.

He saw a ladder in the middle of the room that led to some sparking wires. He considered climbing the ladder so that he could fix the wires, hoping that would keep the lights on, but he just could not get himself to do it.

He was scared. Everything about the house scared him. As if Barnes hadn't been dealing with enough already, the house developed several ceiling leaks, which caused rainwater to accumulate in the living room.

As he left the living room and entered the kitchen, he passed by the basement door. As he did, he felt a cold chill run up and down his spine. It was the same cold chill he had felt the night they had found the six bodies of the Hamilton family members inside the house. He stopped in front of the door and memories of that night flooded back into his mind. He remembered walking down the basement steps and finding Evie curled up against her mother. He thought about how he had scooped up her little body and had carried her to an awaiting ambulance. Mostly, he remembered the look in her eyes, when she had woken up in the emergency room. They had been helpless to save her.

He heard more sounds, which caused him to wake from his dreadful trip down memory lane. The sounds were coming from the basement. Jay and Katie heard his footsteps. They yelled for help. He grasped the doorknob. It was ice cold. His hand froze to the doorknob. From behind him, the living room's chandelier dropped from the ceiling. The lights went out. He was not able to move. He could not see the dangers that were around him.

The floor became flooded, and wires were sparking. Wires came down from the ceiling, wrapped around his waist, and pulled at him. At that moment, It appeared to Barnes in Its long, black robe. Half of Its skeletal face could be seen under Its hood. It used Its cloven hoof to kick Barnes's hand from the doorknob, shattering three of his fingers. Barnes yelled in pain. His yell was so loud it echoed throughout the house. The wires still kept twisting around him, wrapping around his neck, and suspending him above the floor.

The house is trying to kill me, he thought. No, It

was killing him. He finally knew what had happened to those people. A mysterious creature in a long, black robe and with a cloven hoof and skeletal face had taken their lives. *What is It thinking?*

He had become delusional. None of it seemed real. None of it seemed possible. He wondered what was happening to him. Was he dying? He wondered what was making the sounds in the basement. Were there people down there who needed his help? All of these thoughts were racing through his head. His thoughts slowed until only two remained: *What is It? Where did It come from?*

It stood looking at him as death took him away. Finally, the wires rested on the wet floor next to Officer Barnes's body and the fallen chandelier.

The house fell eerily silent. Jay and Katie knew that their help was gone. Katie sat down and began to cry. She felt overwhelmed by everything that had happened. Jay put his arm around her and pulled her close to him. She laid her head upon his chest and wept for what seemed like a very long time. She didn't know what to say, so she stayed there and felt lost and empty.

She needed Jay to lift her up, to give her hope, and to make her want to continue this fight. Just as she was thinking that, he whispered to her, "Katie, I know how you feel right now, but we can't give up. Our friends wouldn't want us to do that. We owe it to them to keep trying."

"I don't know what else we can do," she replied.

"I'm going to try to move these bricks," he said, "while you keep reading in the book. There has to be something in there that can help us."

He helped her to her feet. She turned to walk toward the book, but Jay pulled her back. He looked into her eyes. He glanced down at her lips and then back to her eyes again. He used one hand to cup her face and pulled it close to his. He kissed her on the lips, smoothly and romantically, letting her know that he was sincere and committed to getting through the night together.

She returned that kiss, acknowledging that she would be by his side for the nightlong fight against whatever It might be. With her hands on his chest, she leaned her head against his chin for a few more seconds of reassurance. Then she slowly pulled away to go to the book and read from it. Jay began moving bricks and debris as quickly as possible, without causing a worse slide or cave-in.

Katie read descriptions of other witches, warlocks, and demons. Sometimes, she read stories in the book that described battles among them. If the book described the witches being defeated, it also told the story of how it had been done.

One witch named Mortica put death spells on anyone who crossed her in any way. She practiced black magic. She had sold her soul for eternal life. There didn't seem to be any information on how to defeat her or to avoid death from one of her spells. Katie took that to mean that either the coven had never had a run-in with her, or it had never learned how to defeat her.

One warlock named Wheldor had the power to create balls of energy that could be used as weapons against his enemies. Sadly, he saw even women and children as enemies if they crossed his path while he was in a foul mood. The warlock had been defeated by the coven when it had turned one of his own energy balls against him.

A demon named Syan was capable of taking the life of any person who made the comment or even had the thought of wishing for his or her own death. He was capable of granting the wish, whether that person really meant it or not. He would take a life in a painful way, and the individual's soul would be condemned for eternity. This demon was defeated when the coven tricked him into wishing for his own death. The Garrison family's powerful three sisters had then used a spell to cast him back into the pit of hell and bind him so that he could never return.

While Katie found all of this information to be interesting, it wasn't really helping her. She closed the book, feeling helpless once again. "My ancestors knew how to use this book and what all of this meant, but I was never taught any of this by my grandmother or mother," Katie told Jay. "If any of my ancestors could help me now, I wish they would." At those words, the book flew open to a page with a title that read, "It That Has No Name."

"If this is the demon that has been after us tonight, we need to know everything we can about it," Katie said. She and Jay gathered around the book. The gentle rain outside had turned into a storm. The electricity in the house had gone out, but Jay and Katie had plenty of light because of their lanterns and candles. The basement was cold and damp. Jay made sure every lantern was lit, and then he wrapped his arms around Katie to help keep her warm.

"It That Has No Name is an upper-level demon, which was never given a name by Satan, to prevent It from having that as a weakness," Katie read. "It is seated at Satan's right hand and does his work: capturing souls by preying on the fears of Its victims."

"The book says It is capable of assuming the image of any person or thing that It desires and is capable of moving any object in any way It chooses," Jay said.

"It is said to have no definite form, but the image of a tall, dark figure in a hooded, black robe with a skeletal face and a cloven hoof has been repeatedly seen and documented over the decades," Katie read.

"That's what I saw," she said, turning to look at Jay who was looking over her shoulder.

"Me too," he said. "Listen, we're getting really close to this thing. Be careful. Expect something to happen at any time now."

"This demon preys on our fears," she said. "How are we supposed to overcome that?"

"What else does the book say?" Jay asked.

"It says that sometimes, only the victim sees and experiences the attack and that others can't see what is happening. All they see is the effect of the attack afterwards," Katie said. "Then there is a poem."

"Read it," Jay said.

Katie read,

> It whispers from the darkness.
> It calls out your name.
> It enters your mind.
> It drives you insane.
>
> It knows your darkest secrets.
> It uses them to take you down.
> It sees into the depths of your soul.
> It watches as you drown.
>
> It steals your breath with just one look.
> It captures your soul with its left hook.
> It breaks your bones with its right hoof.
> It won't leave you alone once it is hooked.
>
> It can smell your fear,
> Taste your tears,
> Hear your cries,

> Rip out your soul,
> And then you die.
>
> Nothing stops the No Name, no.
> Nothing stops the No Name, no.

"Nothing stops it. Is that what it says? Is that really what it says, Katie?" Jay asked.

She nodded. "It must have been written by one of my ancestors," Katie said.

Tears welled up in her eyes. She hugged Jay tightly. Now she believed that there had to be something else inside the book that would help them. She pulled away to go read from it, but Jay pulled her back. "I just wanna hold you," Jay said and then kissed her on her forehead.

Katie knew nothing else to do but hug him and grasp her necklace. It had been given to her by her grandmother on her sixteenth birthday. A beautiful cross with a small opal adorned her neck. She wore it all the time. The opal was a symbol for hope, so it was quite fitting that she was wearing it on this night.

It was growing late now, but no one was going to miss them until morning. All they could do was wait for It to play Its next hand. They would fight as hard as they could for as long as they could. The one thing they knew for sure was that they were not letting go of each other.

18

HELP IS ARMED FOR BATTLE

Baker arrived at the hospital to find out about the autopsy of Melanie Holcomb. He passed Dr. Jameson in the emergency room hallway, as he was making his way toward the morgue. Both men nodded at each other. They had barely spoken since the death of little Evie. Now once again, they found themselves working together on a mysterious night under peculiar circumstances.

Just as the detective was about to reach the morgue, he heard his name called by another doctor in the hospital. "Detective Baker, how are you, sir?" Dr. Carrollton asked.

"I'm well, doctor, and you and your family?" the detective asked.

"We're well. Thank you for asking," the doctor said.

"What brings you to our great hospital in such bad weather?"

"A single-vehicle accident, I'm afraid," the detective said.

"Oh, how many lives were lost?" the doctor asked.

"Um, how did you know that?" the detective asked.

The doctor pointed toward the sign by the door. "You're standing outside the morgue, detective," Carrollton said.

"Oh, yes, of course. Only one. A teenage girl," Baker said. "Did your daughter know a Melanie Holcomb?"

"Know her? That is Katie's best friend. Is she the girl who was killed in the accident?" the doctor asked.

The detective said, "Yes, it was her. Very young. So sad to see—"

"And there were no other teenagers involved in the accident?" the doctor said. He expressed worry and concern.

"No, none. Why?" asked the detective.

"Because my daughter was supposed to be spending the night at her house tonight," the doctor replied.

"Officer Barnes could have a lead on a place where some kids might have been holding a party," Baker said. "Let me check with him." Baker called Barnes, but there was no response. "I know where Officer Barnes was headed. Let me go check it out. I will get back to you as soon as I know something," the detective said.

"There is no reason to get all worked up just yet. We don't know that she is in any danger."

"Forgive me, detective, but my daughter may be missing. That is enough for me to get worked up over," the doctor responded.

"I understand, but I will call you as soon as I check it out," he said.

"I'm sorry, detective, but I'm going with you to check it out. I won't just sit here and wait to hear from you," Carrollton said decisively.

He called his wife. "Christina, didn't you tell me that Katie was spending the night at Melanie Holcomb's house?" the doctor asked.

"Yes, she is staying with Melanie. Why? What's wrong?" Christina asked. "I can hear the concern in your voice."

"There has been an accident, Christina," he said.

"Oh, dear God," she said.

"Melanie has been in a car accident," he elaborated. "She's dead."

"Oh, no! Poor Johnathan. He must be devastated. What about Katie? Where is she? Is she safe?" she asked.

"Katie may be missing. She wasn't in the car," he said.

"What do we do? We need to find Katie. I should start by calling Johnathan and Katie's friends," she said.

"Remain calm, Christina," he said. "We don't know that she is in danger. I'm with Detective Baker now.

He and Officer Barnes were going to check out a place where there was supposed to be a party tonight. Tristan's dad, Officer Templeton, told them that the kids had a big party planned. I'm going to ride with Baker. I will call you as soon as I know something."

"Be careful, David," she said.

Both of Katie's parents were obviously distraught. Christina spent her time trying to reach Melanie's father and Katie's friends by phone and staying busy in her kitchen while she awaited word from her husband. Carrollton rode along with Baker. He hoped to find that Katie had only made the teenage mistake of sneaking out with friends and that she was safe.

When Christina reached Johnathan by phone, she told him that she was so sorry for his loss and that Melanie would be missed. He asked her why Melanie had gone out on Highway 89, and Christina informed him that she did not know the reasons why. She asked him why he thought she might know the answer, and he replied that Melanie was supposed to have been staying the night at her house with Katie. Christina informed Johnathan that Katie had told her that she was spending the night with Melanie. Realizing that they had both been lied to, they ended their call. Katie really was missing.

"Is there something going on with Katie?" James asked.

"Katie? Why would you ask that?" his mother said.

"I don't know," James said. "You seem really worried. That's all."

Christina noticed that he failed to make eye contact with her and came across as a little disingenuous. She knew that she needed to question him further. "James, it is very important for you to tell me if you know anything about your sister," she stated. She believed he knew something that he was hiding from her.

"No, I don't know anything," he said. "She is just staying overnight at Melon Pop's house. I mean Melanie's."

"What if I told you that I already knew she was not with Melanie? What if I told you that something terrible happened tonight and that Katie could be in trouble or in danger?" she said. She spoke with such genuine concern that James knew that it must be true.

"I might know something about where Katie is spending the night tonight," he said.

"James, you must tell me right now," she ordered.

"Katie and Melanie needed a place to hold their first senior party, and I kind of gave them an idea of a place to do it," he said.

"Where, James, where?" his mother demanded.

"The house you showed us out on Highway 89," he replied.

"I have to call your father," Christina said. "I will deal with you later." She called her husband on his cell phone.

171

"David, Katie may be in the house I purchased through our realty company out on Highway 89," she said.

"Do you mean the one you're having remodeled?" Carrollton asked.

"Yes," she responded hurriedly.

"Detective Baker said that we're headed to a house out on Highway 89. I bet it's the same house," Carrollton said.

"You won't have cell phone service once you get to the outskirts of town," she reminded him. "I can't just sit here. I will meet you there."

"Christina, be careful," he said.

They ended their phone call.

Not knowing what they might find once they reached the house out on Highway 89, Christina called her mother, Rebecca. "Mom, I need to leave James with you tonight. May I bring him over?" Christina asked.

"Yes, of course. What's wrong, Christina?" Rebecca asked.

"I can't explain right now, Mom, but Katie may be in some trouble. I need to meet David out on Highway 89," Christina said. "I'm already on my way to you."

"What kind of trouble? Where on Highway 89? Where is David?" Rebecca asked inquisitively.

"It's the house I bought and am remodeling," Christina said.

"Christina, I think I should go with you," Rebecca added. "You know I grew up in that house, and it has a history."

"What kind of history, Mother? You keep telling me that I shouldn't have bought the house because of its past, but you never elaborate about what you know," Christina said. "I know about the unexplained deaths, rumors, and folklore. I'm pulling up to your house now." She hung up.

"Why don't you come inside for a few minutes?" Rebecca asked as she came to the car.

"Katie might not have a few minutes, Mother," Christina said. "Melanie was killed in a car accident tonight. Katie is missing."

"Melon Pops is dead?" James asked. He was shocked by what he heard.

"Then we will get into your car, and I will explain on the way," Rebecca said.

"No, Mom. I don't want James there. Please just keep him here," Christina said.

"Okay, I will, but Christina, please put on your armor. Believe in the only real power of three—the Holy Trinity. Take this," Rebecca said as she hung a rosary around Christina's neck.

"I have prayed, mom. I have faith everything will be alright," Christina said.

"Okay, I will keep James safe," Rebecca said. "Just take my word on one thing. Don't let Katie talk to the police this evening about anything she experienced tonight. She may need time to process everything about this night before she talks to them. Just bring her home safely. Now, go to her!"

Christina pulled away wondering why her mother thought she needed to keep James safe and what the police might want to discuss with Katie. Wasn't James already safe? Wasn't staying out all night a matter for parents to resolve? Then she pushed these thoughts away, believing she was overthinking what had been said. It was time for her to focus on Katie. How could Katie have done this? She was shocked by Katie's actions and even more surprised that James had known about it and had not said something to her. None of that mattered right now. What mattered now was to make sure that Katie and anyone else involved was safe.

Christina thought about Melanie's father. She wondered what he must be feeling at the loss of his child. She was such a beautiful, smart, and talented young lady. Her loss would be deeply felt, not only by her family but also in her school and community. She had been deeply involved in many school activities and community events. She had just finished helping with the hospital's annual walk-a-thon to raise money for the pediatric cancer patients' playroom. That was just her personality. She loved everyone.

By now, she had crossed into the area where cellular service was no longer available. Carrollton and Baker had done so as well. Baker could not reach Barnes by radio either. All communication was failing them. They were on their own.

19 GOOD VERSUS EVIL, LIGHT VERSUS DARK

Jay kept Katie warm, wrapped up in his arms. Katie had never thought about Jay the way she was thinking about him right then. She could hardly believe that she was thinking about anything other than how to get out of there before It returned. It may not have a name, but at least they now knew what It was: a demon.

Even though they knew this, she wasn't frightened anymore. She felt very safe, so she settled in even closer to Jay as he opened his arms a little wider to get a stronger grip around her. When she felt the muscles in his arms tense up, she stroked them with her hands to feel the strength in them. She leaned her body against his. The room was damp and cold, but there was heat building between them.

Jay breathed on her neck. She tilted her head to the

side to encourage him to kiss her, so he did. He kissed down her neck. She turned around in his arms and pressed against him. He kissed her multiple times. He pulled her leg up onto his leg. She lifted up her other leg and then wrapped both of them around his waist. He leaned her against the table, continuing to kiss her lips and neck.

She wondered how she could be thinking about him like this right now. But she was, and she couldn't help that she longed to touch him and to feel him touch her. She lightly touched her fingertips to his chest and down to his abdomen. She felt the wounds he had suffered that night. He reached down to remove her shirt, saw her necklace, and paused.

He cared too much for her to continue. He could not get himself to go any further. She removed her shirt herself and pressed against him. She leaned upward, and they kissed. She wanted him, and she couldn't help how she felt.

Suddenly, Jay gasped, and his back straightened. Katie asked what was wrong but got no response. Jay dropped to his knees and then fell forward onto the floor. Katie knew something was happening to him that she could not see. It was there somewhere. It had been watching them.

"Leave him alone," Katie yelled as she pulled her shirt back on. "We're not afraid of you."

Unbeknownst to Katie, Jay had a fear of needles,

and he had been stabbed in the back by about twenty one-and-a-half-inch syringes. Jay struggled to get to his feet and began to dig at the debris pile. "Katie, we have to keep trying to get out," he said. "Keep digging. It's our only chance."

Jay saw It. It was standing in the shadows in a corner of the room. It was only a matter of time before It tortured both of them. Their only chance was to try to get away. They did not have enough knowledge to stand and fight against the demon.

Katie started removing debris as fast as she could. Then she saw the pain in Jay's face. She could see the slash marks on his arms. She didn't know how Jay managed to move the debris. She took two steps toward him, but he put up his hand to stop her. He yelled at her. "Katie, that's what It wants. Just keep digging. It's the only way," he struggled to say.

Katie wanted nothing more than to be by his side and help him, but he didn't want her help. He wanted her to keep digging, so that is what she did. She kept her eyes on him though. She couldn't help it. She knew he must be in incredible pain, and that hurt her deeply. Getting Jay out of there alive was her goal now. Losing him was not an option. She became more motivated and began working harder.

Soon she could see through to the other room. Jay helped her move some more bricks and debris to clear the way into the main basement storage room. Just as they almost finished, It turned Jay, while he still had the last few bricks in his hand, and suspended him in midair.

Katie was not able to see how he was being suspended in the air, but she knew the demon was responsible for it. She also knew that she was not leaving that room without Jay. She tried to grab Jay and pull him down. She heard deep, roaring laughter just before Jay was thrown against the wall, hitting it hard.

She tried to run to him, but It pulled her backward by her hair. It pulled her close so that It could smell her. It behaved as though something about her was familiar to It. Katie fought It. She kicked and punched. It was not fazed by her attack. She tried to run from It, but It just held her by the waist.

She couldn't take any more. She knew that the book said It fed on their fears. She didn't know what fears she had. The only one right now was that It was going to kill Jay and that she would lose him forever. A million thoughts raced through her mind all at once.

Then, suddenly, her mind was clear, and she heard her grandmother's voice in her head. "Know from where your strength comes, my dear," Rebecca said to her. "There is only one thing in this life to fear."

"Thank you, Grandma," Katie whispered.

Katie understood what her grandmother meant the moment that she heard her. The demon was holding her by her hair and waist. She reached up and yanked her necklace from her neck. Holding it up, she pressed the cross with its opal stone against the claws that held her by the waist. The demon yanked Its arm back and let her go.

When It did this, the room filled with bats, which circled her and Jay. Many of them landed on Jay, and they began to feed on his blood. Katie fought the bats, which were landing in her hair. As soon as she got them away from her, she yelled as she ran toward Jay to get them off him. Her yell caused them to go. She had somehow accessed the power of her ancestors and the power of her faith in God. She had been able to use it to fight the demon. She turned to face It. It sank into the shadows of the room.

She knew the demon wasn't gone and was just waiting for another opportunity to fight her. Quickly, It came from out of the shadows. It rammed her. She flipped up, over It, and onto the floor, which caused her necklace to fall from her hand. It believed she was defenseless until she challenged It and showed the power and the strength that she did not know she had. She stood up and confronted the demon. It knew that her weakness was Jay, so It reached over and threatened to harm him.

"You don't frighten me, demon," she yelled. It reached over and peeled back layers of skin from Jay's chest. "You want me, demon? Take on the image of my fear. Become my fear. I fear only one thing, demon, and it's not you!"

The demon shuddered. The demon reached out for her but stumbled backward. With each attempted advance, It found Itself farther away from her. It began to change forms so rapidly that Katie could not make out a single one. She only knew that It wasn't able to assume the form of her greatest fear, for she was a God-fearing Christian.

A portal opened in the basement wall, and the demon made Its way toward it. You could hear the screams of those who were suffering in pain and agony coming from the portal. Katie could see into the portal. The walls were lined with human body parts, fire, lava, and metal blades.

The demon stepped through the portal in an effort to escape an impending defeat. While crossing through it, the demon made Its last effort to prevail. He made a long slithering-tongued low-level demon grab Katie by the leg, causing her to fall to the floor. The low-level demon dragged her toward the portal. She reached out and tried to grab anything she could so that she wouldn't be dragged across the line that separated hell from her world. There was nothing to grab. Everything was just out of reach.

She was about to panic when her hand felt something that she could grasp, and then she felt relieved. She closed her fist around the necklace and held it tightly.

She aimed it at the portal. Nothing happened. She thought for sure that the power of God would close the portal.

Now, she was halfway through the portal. She was in it up to her waist. The arms of those who had passed through it before her were pulling on her. She realized that they were souls trapped in hell and felt sorry for them. The metal blades were cutting her jeans, and she could feel the heat from the fire that burned around her. The portal seemed to get smaller and smaller with each inch she was pulled through it.

She touched the low-level demon's tongue with her necklace, and it let go of her. She used all of her strength to pull herself out of the portal. It That Has No Name was coming back after her. Just as It put Its cloven hoof through the portal, Katie put her necklace just inside the edge of the portal and bowed her head. Just like that, the portal closed.

She was lying on the floor in the silence of the dark basement. She turned toward the portal and saw that a piece of the demon's cloven hoof had been cut off on the basement side of the portal when it had closed. She picked it up and looked at the place where the portal had been. Breathing heavily, she said, "I name you Defeated."

It was so dark. Even the candles had burned out. She had to find Jay. His body had dropped to the floor when the portal had closed. She called to him but received no response. She felt along the floor where his body should have been until she felt his leg. She felt her way to his face. He was unconscious and did not respond to her. He had lost so much blood.

She placed her hand on his chest to see if he was breathing. Then she put her hand under his nose to feel for air moving in and out. He was not breathing. She felt for a pulse. She had lost him.

"No, no, no, no, no!" she cried. "We won! We beat it! You can't leave me." She lifted up his head and shoulders and held him. She leaned in close to whisper in his ear, "Don't leave me, Jay. Don't leave me."

20 KATIE'S POWER AWAKENS

Arriving just outside the house, Baker and Carrollton approached with caution. They began calling out for the kids immediately, hoping they would receive a response. From a quick review of the exterior, the detective noticed several cars parked near the left side of the house. Baker asked Carrollton if he recognized his daughter's car. Carrollton replied that he did.

They went to the front door. It would not open. Baker attempted to kick in the door and failed, but Carrollton gave it a try and succeeded. They walked inside, found the lights were out, and used flashlights. Flashbacks of that night in 1990 raced through Baker's head. As they approached the living room, they found Barnes lying on the wet floor. A broken chandelier with its wires sticking out lay on the floor. Baker checked for a pulse. He felt the pain of losing an old friend and colleague.

"Damn, man, no! How could this happen?" Baker said. "Why did you come in here by yourself? You should have called for backup before comin' in this house."

Baker asked Carrollton if he could determine the cause of death. "It appears as though he was electrocuted by these exposed wires on the chandelier when it fell onto this wet floor," Carrollton said. "I'm confused though because Christina has been renovating this house, and most of the house was finished. How could this have happened?"

"Well, the power is out now," Baker said.

Baker spoke to Carrollton, and at first, Carrollton did not hear him. Baker said again, "You need to refocus. Katie could be here and might need your help."

Baker showed him Barnes's hand. It was missing three fingers. "Does electrocution cause that?" Baker asked. Carrollton shook his head.

Using the flashlights to scan the room from where they were kneeling, Baker discovered another body a few feet away from them. It was Chase Monroe's body. The boy had already made a name for himself on the town's high school football team. Carrollton felt his neck for a pulse and shook his head.

"What about a possible cause of death on this one?" Baker asked.

"Broken neck, if I'm guessing. It looks like every bone in his body was broken," Carrollton said.

They began calling Katie's name and the names of any friends Carrollton knew. They entered the living room and found Sandy's body lying on the couch. After checking for a pulse, Carrollton recommended an autopsy for cause of death.

They approached the stairs leading to the second floor, and Baker decided that he would go first. Because the only light was from their flashlights, they could not cover the area quickly. They planned to check each room, one by one. They started with the first room on the right. The detective entered first and immediately saw Gloria's body. They ran to her to offer assistance, but they were too late. She had been dead for a few hours. The cause of death was unknown once again.

Baker could tell that Carrollton was becoming impatient after Carrollton said, "I have to find Katie one way or another." Baker watched as he began running from room to room looking for her. Baker tried to keep up with him. The doctor called out for his daughter, but they heard no response. Baker feared they would not find her alive. They went back down the stairs and searched the main level but found nothing but bottles of alcohol everywhere.

The doctor was about to head out to the pool area when the detective said that there was one more level to check in the house. He told the doctor that the house had a basement.

Meanwhile, Katie heard sounds coming from upstairs: voices and footsteps. She laid Jay's head gently down on the floor and went to the hole in the brick wall. The sounds upstairs became louder. *Help is here,* she thought. She called out to them. "Help! I'm down here! Please, we need help down here!"

"Listen," Baker said.

"That's Katie!" Carrollton said. "She's alive. We have to find her."

They went to the basement door. Her voice was louder. They ran down the stairs and found the body of Robbie. Carrollton reached down to check for a pulse but was certain from the gruesome look of his body that he was no longer alive.

Baker located the hole from which Katie was yelling and began to move even more bricks and fallen debris to enlarge the hole. Carrollton joined him. Carrollton went through the hole and into the room. He hugged Katie and looked her over, up and down, for any injuries. "Katie, are you hurt?" Carrollton asked.

"Dad, I'm okay, but Jay is hurt badly. He needs you, Dad. Hurry!" Katie said.

Outside, Katie's mother had just arrived and now entered the house. "David? Detective Baker? Where are you?" she yelled.

"Down in the basement, Mom. Down here," Katie

responded. Katie continued to yell until her mother heard her. Christina reached for the basement doorknob and found that it was unusually cold, so much so that it distracted her for a moment. Christina refocused and ran down the stairs to the basement. She searched until she found Katie near the entrance to the secret room. Katie and her mother hugged each other.

"Are you okay? I couldn't see anything with the power out. I had to feel along the upstairs walls to find the basement door once I heard your voice. I can't see anything down here," her mother said. "What is going on? What are you doing down here?"

"Mom, things are really bad—really bad," Katie said. "Jay is hurt. I don't think he is going to make it, Mom."

"Oh my God! I'm so sorry, Katie," her mother said.

"Dad is with him now," Katie said.

Baker and Carrollton came back through the entrance to the secret room. Carrollton shook his head at Katie. She yelled that it could not be true and went back into the room to be by Jay's side. Carrollton tried to stop her but failed to do so. Christina stopped him from going after her.

"But we could still be in danger here, Christina," Carrollton said.

"Give her just a minute. We can give her that," Christina replied.

"You don't know what has happened here. There

are many dead kids, Christina, and no explanation of how they died," Carrollton said.

"What happened here?" she said.

"I'm hoping your daughter is going to be able to explain that to us, Mrs. Carrollton," Baker said. "I need to drive about five miles back toward town to make a radio call to get an ambulance and some police investigators out here to work this crime scene. Cellular service is not available out here."

"Crime scene?" Christina said. "How do you know a crime has been committed? This could have been an accident."

"Until I know what happened here, this is a crime scene, and we will collect every piece of what appears to be evidence as a part of this investigation," Baker said.

Katie heard what Baker said, and like Evie so many years earlier, she knew she needed to protect her family's secret. She grabbed the book and as many articles as she could put inside it and covered it with an old towel so that she could carry it out under her arm unnoticed. She also grabbed the piece of the demon's hoof. She didn't want that to become part of Baker's evidence file.

She kneeled down and gave Jay one final kiss on the lips. His lips were so cold. She touched the rest of his body. He was cold all over. The whole basement had started to feel cold again but not freezer-cold like Jay's skin was. Something didn't seem right. She whispered to him, "I love you, Jay."

She stood up and collected herself so that she would be able to carry those items out of the house unnoticed. She walked out of the secret room and up the stairs before she yelled back to her mother, "Let's go, Mom, please. I just want to get out of here. I want to go home."

They had been so busy talking among themselves in the dark that she had been able to walk right by them without them even noticing her. The detective raised objections to her going home before he had a chance to interrogate her about what had happened that night. Memories of what had happened to his last survivor remained in his head. Katie's father insisted that she be checked out at the hospital for a possible concussion and for all of the cuts she had. Her mother was content to take Katie home because that was what Katie wanted to do.

"Tomorrow will be a better day for her to speak to you, Detective Baker," Christina said. "I will bring her to your office myself."

"First thing in the morning!" he responded.

"Agreed," she replied.

"I will check on her cuts at home," Christina told her husband.

Katie and her mother went upstairs and outside. Detective Baker and Carrollton followed them.

"Young lady, I need to know one thing before you leave. Who did this?" the detective asked.

"Detective, please, tomorrow," Christina said.

"This is important," Baker said. "I could have a murderer on the loose."

"All I saw was someone in a long, black robe in a skull mask. That's all I know," Katie said. "Now may I please go home?" The detective replied reluctantly that she could go. Christina and Katie got into the car and left.

When Katie got home, she ran straight to her room to hide the book, despite the calls from her mother.

"Katie! Katie, come down here right now!" her mother demanded.

Katie came down the stairs.

"Is there anything you want to talk about?" her mother asked.

"No, Mom, I really just want to go to bed," she said, "if that's okay with you."

"Well, I guess if you're sure you're doing okay," Christina said. "Let me take a look at those cuts first." Christina tended to Katie's cuts. "Just know I'm here for you if you need to talk or need a hug."

"Yes, Mom. I love you," Katie said.

Katie hugged her mother and went upstairs to her room, where she pulled out the book to write in it. She felt obligated to add her story to its pages for her descendants.

She turned to the page titled "It That Has No Name." She wrote that the demon had opened a portal to hell that had been closed by her necklace with the cross and the opal stone and her request for help from the Holy Trinity. She wrote that the demon had a cloven hoof and that a piece of it had been broken off when the portal had closed. She laid the piece of Its hoof on the book, and like magic, it became part of the book. She was beginning to understand the power of her ancestors and the power of this book.

Katie wondered, *why was this power kept from me all these years? What reason did my grandmother have for not wanting me to know that I was part of a world that was so much bigger than I knew about?* Katie didn't know the answers, but she would sure ask her grandmother as soon as she could.

Christina called her mother after sending Katie off to bed. "I let her come home without answering any questions from the police, Mother, but I'm not sure why you insisted that was important," she said.

"Trust your mother," Rebecca responded. "I have a lot of explaining to do in due time." They ended their conversation with a promise that more information would be shared sooner rather than later.

Katie fell into a deep sleep that night. In her dream, she relived the events of that awful night. She saw her friends' deaths, which she had been helpless to prevent. She watched all of them as they suffered and died at the hands of the demon. She felt the emotion building up inside her.

She awoke to find that she had created a beautiful

red ball of energy, which was now in the palm of her hand. She breathed heavily, and the ball grew bigger with the anger she felt. The light from the glowing ball lit up the room and revealed the silhouette of a figure seated in the chair across from her bed. Without thinking, she threw the ball of energy toward the figure. It took the hit. It must have hurt a lot because it made a sound, which was somewhat familiar to her. She recognized it. She called out in the darkness of the room, "Jay?"

"Shh, I'm here," he responded.

"But how? I felt you myself. You were so cold," she said. She was confused by his presence.

"That doesn't matter now," he replied. "I just wanted you to know that I heard you."

"Heard what?" she asked.

"I heard you say that you love me," he said, moving to look into her eyes. "I wanted to tell you that I love you too." He kissed her on the lips. His lips were as cold as they had been when she had last kissed him.

"You're still so cold."

"I will be okay. Just knowing you're safe makes everything okay."

"What about you? Are you safe? Are you okay?" she inquired.

"Things will not be the same for me now. I'm not the same now," he said.

"What does that mean? Let me help you. I'm

learning about the power of the craft. It's real, and you know how much I believe in prayer," she said.

"I saw your handy work just now. That ball of energy wasn't too bad for being half-asleep when you created it," he said and then laughed at her.

"Don't laugh. I'm serious," she said.

"None of that can change things for me now. I am what I am," Jay stated.

"What does that mean?" she demanded.

"I have to go now," he said. "Charles is going to help me through this new life. You will remember him in due time."

"What new life? Does this mean you won't be waking up at home tomorrow like me? I'm scared for you."

"Don't be. I will always be with you," he said, kissed her on the cheek, and jumped from her window.

"Wait!" she said and gasped. She jumped from the bed, went to the window, and looked out, but he was gone. She turned back to the book. Its pages were turning wildly until it finally stopped on one page. She walked from the window to the book. She read as the words appeared on the page,

> Jay: vampire, created by vampire bats that were unleashed by a high-level demon during Its attack on humans. The vampire feeds on human blood. Its soul

is condemned to hell once it murders a human for its blood. To protect yourself from a vampire, you may use a circle of salt, garlic, or a cross. To kill a vampire, you must drive a wooden stake through its heart.

She sunk to the floor. The bats that had become tangled in her hair had not bitten her. Now, she almost wished they had. She longed to be with Jay. Her heart was broken.

Over the next week, Katie was questioned multiple times by police officers. They were trying to find a man in a long, black robe with a skull mask who had committed seven gruesome murders at a crime scene that also resulted in one accidental death. She attended funerals for six friends and one police officer during that first week.

In a crazy twist of events, the body of Jay Newsome went missing from the morgue on the night of the incident, and it was never recovered. After three weeks, his parents decided to hold a memorial service for him and establish a grave marker in the cemetery. They hoped that his body would be recovered one day. Katie felt Jay's presence on the day of that graveside service. She knew he was there watching them. He could see them grieving for him, and she could feel that he was grieving too. However, he was not able to be there to feel the support of his family and friends. That made her hurt even more for him.

All she could think of was seeing him again. In that moment, she saw some movement in the shadows near the trees and felt that she might have more control over his return than she had originally thought.

ABOUT THE AUTHOR

P. S. Kessell has a master's degree in educational administration from Texas A&M University, Texarkana. She has previously published another book titled, *From A to Z on Instructional Strategies*, which is a creative way to introduce students to Common Core state standards.

She has one son, James, and one daughter, Breanna. She enjoys living near her family and friends in Fishersville, Virginia.

Her book *It That Has No Name* is the first in a series of horror stories based upon some of the same characters. Her love for horror, her interest in the supernatural, and her faith in God combine to create an original work of fiction.

Her other interests include reading, writing poetry, spending evenings with good friends, and vacationing in Mexico, a place she considers her home away from home.

CPSIA information can be obtained
at www.ICGtesting.com
Printed in the USA
LVHW092307270323
742785LV00015B/828